"I think you're being rather premature in drawing your conclusions about me, Mario.

"We've barely known each other for more than a couple of weeks." His hands were still on her shoulders and Fleur was suddenly conscious of his touch.

"Has it really only been two weeks?" The genuine bewilderment in his voice made her look up. "I feel I have known you so much longer."

Her mind drifted back to last night on the balcony and the emotions that had coursed through her then. Could so much have happened for them both in such a short space of time?

CAROL MARINELLI is a nurse who loves writing. Or is she a writer who loves nursing? The truth is Carol's having trouble deciding at the moment, but writing definitely seems to be taking precedence! She's also happily married to an eternally patient husband (an essential accessory when panic hits around chapter six) and is mother to three fabulously boisterous children. Add a would-be tennis player, an eternal romantic and a devout daydreamer to that list and that pretty much sums Carol up. Oh, she's also terrible at housework….

The ITALIAN'S TOUCH

CAROL MARINELLI

MEDITERRANEAN PASSIONS

TORONTO • NEW YORK • LONDON
AMSTERDAM • PARIS • SYDNEY • HAMBURG
STOCKHOLM • ATHENS • TOKYO • MILAN • MADRID
PRAGUE • WARSAW • BUDAPEST • AUCKLAND

ISBN 0-373-80614-0

THE ITALIAN'S TOUCH

First North American Publication 2003.

Copyright © 2002 by Carol Marinelli.

CHAPTER ONE

'WHAT time do you call this?' Bleary-eyed, Kathy pulled open the front door. 'Whose bright idea was this job share again?'

'Yours,' Fleur said pointedly. 'And next time you have one, please, don't run it by me.'

'You know you can't wait really. Ben's in the living room, watching cartoons.' She smiled at Alex who was nervously clinging to Fleur's leg. 'Time for a cuppa?'

Fleur looked at her fob watch.

'Come on,' Kathy urged. 'You don't want to put the rest of us to shame.'

Realising Alex wasn't going to let her go without a fight, Fleur nodded her acceptance, taking a reluctant Alex through to the lounge before joining Kathy at the kitchen table.

'Getting nervous?' Kathy asked, placing a steaming mug on the kitchen table along with a saucer of chocolate Tim-Tams.

'Terrified,' Fleur admitted, automatically reaching for a biscuit. 'I would have thought toast and Vegemite would be more the go at this hour.'

'It's not every day you go back to work. I'd say chocolate was definitely more appropriate.'

'I'm beginning to wonder what on earth I've taken on,' Fleur said gloomily as her Tim-Tam dissolved into an unsalvagable wreck in her coffee.

'You'll walk it,' Kathy said brightly, pushing the saucer towards Fleur.

'If you tell me it's like riding a bike, I won't be responsible for my actions,' Fleur replied, carefully choosing another biscuit. 'I'm so rusty I'm even struggling to keep up with the medical dramas on television. Maybe I should have done a refresher course.'

'Rubbish,' Kathy said fiercely. 'You've only been away two and a half years, and you're going to have a reorientation program organised by Super-nurse Danny. You told me yourself that you weren't going to be in Resus for a few weeks until you got your confidence back, so what's to know? The sink in the sluice still blocks up. Len the porter is still moaning about his back and Danny ''Mr Unit Manager'' still thinks that he's God's gift to the nursing profession, though I don't know how, considering the fact he spends most of his day in his office. Mind you,' she said lowering her voice, 'there has been a considerable improvement in the EB stakes.'

'EB?' Fleur enquired anxiously. Another thing she didn't know!

'Eligible bachelors. Namely the dashing Mr Mario Ruffini—he's the new visiting consultant I've been going on about. Let me tell you that when God made that man he certainly had his contact lenses in. Mario Ruffini is reason enough to put your lipstick on in the morning. Now before you say, ''But you're a happily married woman,'' I know all that. So happily married, in fact, that I can appreciate a fine specimen when I see one. When you meet him in the flesh you'll see what I mean!'

She glanced over to the clock on the cooker. 'Time you weren't here, I think.'

Fleur never cried—well, almost never and even then only in private—but as she stood to go she felt the sting of moisture as her eyes filled. 'I'm doing the right thing, aren't I, Kathy? With Alex, I mean. He's so clingy at the moment, so scared of any changes…'

Kathy, ever practical, handed her a tissue but, realising a bit more was needed in this instance, enveloped her friend in a warm hug. 'Of course you're doing the right thing, Fleur. It's been over two years since Rory died. It really is time to move on a bit.

'Look, today you start back at work; it's a whole new chapter in your life and just what you and Alex both need. It will force you to cut the cord a bit, so to speak. This is going to be the making of both of you and I truly believe things really are going to get easier now. You'll see.'

And so, after a bit of a last-minute dash, Fleur found herself at handover bang on seven-thirty, feeling rather self conscious in her new uniform, her thick blonde waves tied securely at the nape of her neck. But apart from a couple of anxious stares cast in her direction, on the whole she felt pretty much welcome.

Monday morning in Accident and Emergency, it seemed, hadn't changed one iota. The waiting room was starting to fill and a few patients lay on trolleys in the cubicles, waiting for the ward rounds to be completed, which would hopefully clear the way for them to move from the department into a bed.

'In the observation ward, we currently have two patients.' Moira, the night charge nurse, suppressed a tired yawn. 'Kane Dwyer, eighteen years old, put his hand through a window late last night. He's sobering up and starting to feel very sorry for himself. Currently nil by mouth and first on the theatre list for a tendon repair. Strictly speaking, he's under the orthopaedics, but the beds were full and Mr Richardson gave the OK for him to be held here until he goes to Theatre.'

Fleur listened intently, jotting down the information on a small pad.

'The other patient is Hilda Green, sixty-five, fell at home with query loss of consciousness. No fracture on the X-ray but Mr Ruffini wasn't happy and wanted her to stay overnight. She's for a CT scan this morning.'

Though she was paying attention to all that was being said, Fleur couldn't help but glance over to the empty resus area. The resus area where Rory had been worked on, where she'd kissed him for the last time while he'd still been warm...

'Fleur, perhaps you could take the obs ward this morning. A quiet morning might be the best way to go.' Danny's voice snapped her back to attention.

'Sure,' Fleur replied, relieved at the apparent reprieve from the beastly resus room. 'Is the hand clinic still held there at ten-thirty?'

'Yep, and judging by our theatre book it's going to be a big one. Half of Melbourne must have been stitched up this weekend. I'll send Lucy, the student, in to help you with the clinic. If you need anything in the meantime, don't hesitate to buzz on the intercom.'

Fleur managed a confident grin. 'I'm sure even I can cope with two patients, but thanks.'

'I can smell perfume,' Delorus the night nurse cheerfully declared. 'Which must mean I can go home.' Her ear-to-ear grin stretched even wider when she realised it was Fleur taking over from her. 'Honey, it is *so* good to see you,' she said, grabbing Fleur in a tight embrace. 'You, my darling, are just what this place needs to brighten it up. Things aren't the same here, you'll soon see.'

'Rubbish.' Fleur laughed. 'You just need a holiday.'

'And you need some good food inside you—you're miles too thin. Do you forget to lay a place for yourself when you feed that gorgeous son of yours? I'll have to bring in some of my fried rice and chicken and put some meat on them bones.'

'Delorus, I seem to remember that you thought I was too thin when I was eight months pregnant! But, yes, please, to the rice and chicken—there's always a space in my fridge for your delectable cooking.' Looking around the small ward, Fleur's voice took on a more serious tone. 'How are they?'

'Nothing to report. Moira gave you the handover, I presume? Kane's due for his IV antibiotics at eight—I'll check them with you before I go—and Hilda's neuro obs have all been stable overnight. She's knitting away in her bed and can't wait to get home, like me. Speaking of delectable, Mario is on this morning, and he wants to review Hilda himself after her CT. Now, there's a real man for you, darling, you're in for a treat. I've got a hot date lined up with him soon. He wanted someone to join him while he sampled the delicacies Chinatown has to offer and, honey, I can't wait.'

'Not you as well?' Fleur groaned. 'I'd say you've got a bit of competition there, Delorus.'

Despite the fact Delorus was easily the wrong side of sixty, she pursed her well-painted lips. 'Honey,' she said in a low voice, 'Mario Ruffini is a hot-blooded Italian. They like a woman with good hips, it's in their genes, and I'm sure ahead of the crowd in that department.' Sashaying towards the drug cupboard, she turned and gave Fleur a wicked grin. 'Girl, that HRT was the best thing that ever happened to me.'

They were laughing so hard it took ten minutes to check the drugs when it should have taken two. 'Sweet dreams, Delorus.'

'I sure hope not.' Laughing huskily, Delorus made her way out of the ward.

Happy that the drugs were all checked, Fleur decided to introduce herself to the patients before checking over the paperwork

'Good morning, Mrs Green, I'm Sister Fleur Hadley. How are you feeling this morning?' Fleur smiled warmly as she pulled the curtains around her to give Hilda some privacy. The observation ward tended to be used as a walkway to the kitchen and staffroom during the day, something that had always irritated Fleur.

'Just a bit of a headache, Sister.'

The shiny purple egg on her forehead left Fleur in no doubt that Hilda was an expert in understatement.

'Still,' the patient continued cheerfully, 'it's not bad enough to stop me knitting.'

'What are you making?' Fleur enquired, looking at the small pile of brightly coloured circles on Hilda's bedside table.

'Beanies. I make little hats for the premature babies. It keeps me out of mischief.'

'Well, good on you. I'm just going to do a set of obs and then your breakfast should be here from the kitchen. After your shower you'll be going down for your head CT. Has it all been explained to you?'

'Yes, Mr Ruffini went through everything. He was very kind.'

Fleur found herself waiting for the inevitable, 'Isn't he gorgeous?' But for once it didn't come. Hilda's obs were all satisfactory and, leaving her to her knitting, Fleur made her way over to Kane, who was obviously nervous but doing his best not to show it.

'I'm just going to give you your antibiotics, Kane, and then I'll run through the theatre checklist with you.'

Diligently Fleur checked Kane's ID band against the prescription chart, and though she'd already checked the drugs with Delorus she took a moment to check them again and ask Kane about any allergies. Satisfied everything was in order, she slowly injected the solution into the patient's intravenous bung in his good hand. 'You know you'll be on a different ward once the operation's over?'

'Yeah.' Kane shrugged.

Running through the theatre checklist, Kane continued with his nonchalant demeanour, but when Fleur came to the bit where she asked about any prostheses she saw a glimmer of a smile.

'No, no false teeth.'

'Or a wig?' Fleur asked, giving him a wink. 'And you're not wearing any nail varnish, are you?'

He really grinned this time. 'Not the last time I looked, though I had that much to drink last night you'd probably better check. Who knows what the lads got up to?'

Fleur flicked back the blankets. 'No, you're all right.' She looked up. 'I bet you're not feeling the best, apart from your hand, I mean?'

'I just feel an idiot.' Kane blushed. 'My mum's going to kill me when I get home, she said as much. I don't usually drink, well, not that much anyway. I guess I've learnt my lesson.'

Fleur gave him a sympathetic smile. 'Pretty painful lesson, huh? I'm sure your mum was just upset, but once she's calmed down things will be better. Now, if you need anything, just call. The porters will be here to take you to Theatre soon.'

Very soon, as it turned out. Fleur had just got some paracetamol for Hilda's headache and set up her breakfast tray when the porters arrived with the trolley to take Kane for his operation. As Fleur couldn't leave the ward unattended, she buzzed on the intercom. 'Danny, can you spare someone to take a patient to Theatre or watch the obs ward while I go?'

It was Felicity who came, young and chatty and just the tonic for Kane, Fleur decided. She handed him over, running through the theatre checklist yet again.

'Thanks, Felicity, here's his X-rays. How is it round there?'

'The cubicles are filling but Resus, where I am, is empty. I hope it stays that way.'

'You've just jinxed yourself.' Fleur grinned. 'Good luck, Kane. I'll arrange for a porter to bring your stuff up to the ward.'

Stripping his bed, Fleur placed the linen into the skip and removed the name card above the bed then sorted all Kane's belongings into one of the hospital's blue property bags, deciding not to ring the orderly to wash the bed until Hilda had been discharged.

Collecting a couple of towels and a wash cloth on the way, she walked over to Hilda.

'Mrs Green?' Fleur gently patted her arm. At first glance Hilda appeared to be dozing, her knitting resting in her lap, her glasses on the edge of her nose, but the bottom set of her false teeth was slipping out of her slack mouth and with alarm Fleur noticed her darkening lips.

'Mrs Green!' Fleur's voice was louder, more insistent as she felt for a pulse. Hastily she let the head of the bed down and removed the pillows, grabbing the emergency tray situated on each shelf above the bed. Removing the false teeth which were obstructing Hilda's airway, she deftly inserted a small plastic tube to keep her airway clear and pulled Hilda onto her side, placing an oxygen mask on before making the short dash to the desk and hitting the panic button which would summon help immediately.

Before she'd even made her way back to the bedside a
doctor appeared, immediately sensing the urgency in
Fleur's actions as she raced back to Mrs Green.

'What happened?'

'I was just about to take her for a shower when I found
her unconscious.'

Not waiting for the rest of the staff to appear, he kicked
the brakes off the bed. 'We get her to Resus now.'

The imperfect English and stunning looks could only
mean that this was the man Kathy had been describing.
But there wasn't time for niceties as they pushed the bed
along the highly polished floors, the staff standing back to
let the all-too-familiar sight pass by.

Gliding into Resus, Fleur immediately attached Hilda to
an array of monitors.

'Her oxygen sats are low and her respiration rate is only
six.'

Mario flicked on his torch. 'She's blown a pupil. I'll bag
her—you page the anaesthetist and neurosurgeon.'

A couple more staff had joined them now, working on
the inert body, setting up IV infusions and an intubation
tray. Fleur ran for the telephone and put out the emergency
pages but, replacing the receiver, in that instant it hit her—
it was all too soon, much too soon. 'I'll get Danny.'

'He's in his office and Felicity is up in Theatre. I need
some IV dexamethasone now.'

Like a deer caught in headlights, she stood there for a
second as Lucy rummaged through the drug trolley.

'Now!' Mario demanded more loudly.

Her hands shook as she located the drug. Just preventing
stabbing herself with the needle, she pulled up the solution
into the syringe and handed it to Mario's impatiently out-
stretched hand.

'Run through some IV mannitol.' He looked at the

closed resuscitation doors expectantly. 'Where the hell is the anaesthetist?'

'I only just put out the page,' Fleur replied quickly. 'They'll all be up in Theatre.'

'Then I need you to help me.' Giving Hilda several swift pumps of oxygen, he removed the ambu-bag and slid a laryngoscope into her slack mouth.

'Size seven ET tube.'

Two years ago he wouldn't have needed to ask. The intubation equipment would have been handed to him before he'd even thought it. But this wasn't two years ago, this was today, her first day back...

Shaking, dropping tubes as she frantically located the correct size, she attempted an explanation. 'I'm not supposed to be in Resus, I don't do Resus...'

He looked up, just for a second. The sapphire blue of his eyes seemed out of place with his dark Mediterranean looks, but they were blazing with frustration and anger as he addressed her curtly. 'Then just what the hell are you doing, working in Emergency?'

His words echoed Fleur's thoughts exactly.

'Fleur, what's going on?'

Gratefully she swung round at the sound of Danny's voice. 'My quiet morning just ended.' Glancing over at Hilda lying flat and lifeless, tubes and wires crowding her body, it might just as well have been Rory lying there. Overwhelmed, overwrought, with a sob Fleur fled the room.

'G'day, there, sweetie—time for your morning break?' Beryl, the domestic, made no comment about Fleur's reddened, watering eyes. It happened all too often in this place. 'Why don't youse sit down and I'll bring you a brew? Now, what would you like—a cappuccino or a caffè latte, or just an espresso?'

For a second Fleur thought Beryl was having a joke, but she started when she saw the huge stainless-steel contraption Beryl was lovingly polishing. 'Where on earth did that come from?'

'Dr Mario bought it for us, his first week here. "How am I supposed to function on this slop?" he said, all Latin like, as he threw his coffee into the sink, and that very afternoon here it was. Now, what can I get you?' Beryl showed her the works and in no time the delicious aroma of freshly brewed coffee filled the room as Beryl frothed the milk. 'Just gorgeous,' she said with a small sigh, and Fleur was positive Beryl wasn't referring to the coffee!

Sitting in the empty staffroom, Fleur berated herself over and over. She had been a fool to come back, a fool to think she could just walk in to her old job and carry on as if nothing had happened, when *everything* had changed.

It had seemed such a good idea when Kathy had first suggested it. With the government's latest drive to encourage nurses back into the work force, job share was a concept that had been bandied around like a supposed gift from the gods. Reasonable shifts, flexible rosters, all like manna from heaven for nurses trying to juggle child care and young children. But half the pay with *all* the responsibility, Fleur had pointed out when Kathy had first broached the subject.

'Come on, Fleur,' she'd urged. 'You said yourself, money's a bit tight. And besides, it would do you good to get out a bit more. You know I want to cut back my hours and we'd both have built in babysitters. It's the perfect solution. Heaven knows, they'd welcome you back with open arms—that place has really been going to pot lately. There's just not enough senior staff and morale is really low. It would be great for everyone.'

And after a couple of glasses of wine, well, maybe more than a couple, Fleur had found herself starting to agree.

So now here she was, sitting in the staffroom feeling like the biggest failure in the world. She should never have come back, never have let Kathy talk her into it. Not only was it unfair on the staff, it was downright dangerous for the patients!

In contrast to the first half of the morning, the hand clinic ran smoothly. Danny had been right in his prediction that it would be a big clinic, and patient after patient trooped through—some bandaged, some with slings, others with their injured hands in plastic burn bags. Each hand injury seen in the department was always reviewed the following day, or in this case on the Monday following the weekend. More often than not, a simple re-dressing was all that was required, but in a few cases a more significant problem was detected on review which more than merited the manpower and time that the clinics took. Mario and Luke Richardson, the senior consultant, were both extremely experienced and zipped through the patients. It didn't take long for Fleur to work out that Mario's handwriting was truly appalling and it was far easier to stand behind him and listen, rather than try to decipher his extravagant scrawl after he'd seen the patient.

The next hour was spent in a flurry of taking down dressings, listening to Mario's and Luke's instructions and then re-dressing the injuries. Luke was friendly and professional, but as the clinic carried on Fleur couldn't help but notice a few chips of ice in the cool blue eyes of Mario as he handed her the patients' files. At first she tried to ignore it, sure she was being paranoid, but as the clinic progressed so did Fleur's unease—Mario was definitely upset with her!

Without looking up, he accepted the final patient card from Fleur and read the notes for a moment before addressing the rather unkempt young man sitting at the desk.

'So this was the result of falling off a wall, Jason?'

Fleur watched as Mario gently picked up the grossly swollen hand and examined it carefully.

'Yeah, maybe I got a bit of gravel stuck in it. It's killing me. That medicine the doctor gave me is useless. I don't reckon he knew what he was talking about.'

'I see from Dr Benson's notes that he asked if you might have been bitten.' Mario looked up from the hand to the face of the scruffy young man, who shifted awkwardly in his seat.

'No way, man. Like I said, that doctor didn't know nothing! I fell, I tell you.'

Mario didn't comment straight away, not rising to Jason's aggressive voice. Instead, he slowly turned the hand around. 'The reason that I am...' His forehead creased for a moment. 'How do you say this? Nag,' Mario said finally, obviously pleased with himself at choosing the right word. 'The reason I *nag* is that many people do not realise the harm a small bite can do.'

'I told you, I fell!' Jason was becoming indignant now but Mario chose not to notice as he carried on chatting in an amiable voice. 'Humour me, please, Jason. I need to practise my English.' He flashed a smile and Jason shrugged. 'If, and I hear you when you say no, but *if* this was the result of a bite—say you went to thump someone and their tooth caught your knuckle...'

Jason was seriously rattled now and pulled his hand away but Mario continued unperturbed. 'Then that would make this seemingly simple injury far more serious. A human bite would be far more dangerous than a piece of gravel. You see, a bite acts like a very effective injection, and in this small space...' He flicked his hands dramatically. 'Pow! The germs multiply at a great rate and the hand fills with pus. Of course, if this were a bite, then we would need to admit you and give you intravenous antibiotics. Possibly you would need to go to Theatre to have the wound cleaned to halt the progress of the infection. Anyway, as it is merely from a fall, we don't need to worry as much. We can increase your oral antibiotics and continue with elevation, and I will see you again tomorrow when I hope to see a great improvement. Sister Hadley here will clean it now for you and put it in a high arm sling.' Handing Jason a script, he picked up his patient card and started to write.

Instead of getting up, Jason sat there for a moment. 'Suppose it was a bite and I took the tablets and sling, what would happen then?'

'Well, I really don't think we need to go into that, Jason. I'm sure you are sensible enough that you would tell me so that I could give you the appropriate treatment.'

Jason gave loud sniff. 'Well, come to think of it, I did get mixed up in a bit of a blue on Saturday.'

'A blue?'

Fleur suppressed a smile as Mario tried to work out that particular Australianism. 'A "blue" is a fight, Mr Ruffini.'

Mario glanced around at her. 'Ah, I see. Well, Sister will take you around to the main department and as soon as I finish the clinic we'll see about getting the orthopaedic doctors to admit you.'

'How long will I be in for?' Jason sounded nervous now and nothing like the angry young man of earlier.

'A couple of days probably, but had you left it longer it could have been a lot more serious. I thank you for your honesty, it has made treating you a lot more straightforward.'

Fleur had to hand it to him, Mario certainly had charm. Most doctors—nurses, too, come to that—wouldn't have been able to resist a quick lecture. But Mario had put that aside in the interest of his patient and the result was a positively docile young man now who would get the appropriate care.

'I'd like a swab taken and then could you ask them to put in an IV bung? I'll be around shortly to write up some antibiotics and refer Jason. Thank you, Sister.' He gave a very brief on-off smile without meeting her eyes.

Fleur knew he was annoyed with her and, what was worse, she couldn't blame him. After this morning's debacle he must be wondering what on earth Danny was doing, taking her back!

Jason was soon settled onto a trolley.

'How's the clinic going?' Danny asked

'Fine. We're just about finishing up. Young Jason is to be admitted under the orthopods and needs an IV bung inserted.'

'So it was a bite?' Danny said knowingly. 'He swore blind he'd fallen. How did you get him to open up?'

'Not me,' Fleur admitted. 'Mario forced it out of him, or should I say charmed it out of him.'

'I must say I'm impressed.' Danny laughed. 'So Mario does have his uses after all.'

Fleur gave him a quizzical look.

'Just joking. I know he's a great doctor, he's just thrown the staff into disarray—surely you must have noticed? Lucy is a bumbling wreck whenever he's near, Beryl has given up cleaning and mans the coffee-machine as if she worked in a café and even Len is taking his bad back to see him.'

Fleur laughed but her heart wasn't in it, as she knew what was coming next.

'How are you finding it?'

'The clinic was fine, but I know I lost it a bit this morning. I'm sorry, Danny.'

Danny patted her arm. 'There's no need for that. It was completely understandable.'

'Understandable, yes, acceptable, no.'

'It was just bad luck it had to happen on your first morning. Things will get easier. Anyway, you finish in ten minutes, then you can go home and put your feet up.'

Fleur glanced down at her fob watch. 'Gosh, the morning's flown. How is Mrs Green?' She held her breath, waiting for the answer.

'Still in Theatre. The CT scan showed a massive subdural haematoma. Hopefully once they've evacuated the blood clot she should do well. She wasn't down long.'

'She was fine,' Fleur said, almost to herself. 'It just all happened so quickly.'

'Then it's just as well she was in the observation ward and not at home.'

Fleur nodded. 'I'd better get back and have a quick tidy before I go.'

'Well, I'll see you bright and early tomorrow. Now, don't dwell on it, Fleur. It really is good to have you back.'

By the time she got back, the last patient's injury had been dressed and Lucy was enthusiastically restocking the dressing trolleys. As Fleur joined her, Luke Richardson made his way over, a pile of notes under his arm.

'Thanks for that, Fleur,' he said warmly. 'I must say, I'm glad to see you back. It's nice to have such a busy clinic run so smoothly.' He turned to Mario who was somewhat impatiently hovering, obviously anxious to conclude the conversation. But Luke didn't notice. 'Fleur's one of our finest,' he said enthusiastically.

Mario was obviously choosing to reserve his judgement

and spoke only to the top of her head. 'Indeed,' he said
politely, as Fleur stood there awkwardly. His obvious cool-
ness upset her, and rather surprisingly so. She had been
around long enough to witness more than the occasional
rudeness or indifference from a colleague. But this felt
different. This time it was merited and coupled with the
fact that *everyone* else seemed to get on famously with the
wonderful Mario Ruffini.

Her cheeks burning, Fleur gave the two consultants a
brief smile before making her way to the changing room.

'Damn,' she cursed once the door was safely closed.
Day one and already she'd put someone offside. For a
second she closed her eyes, resting the back of her head
against the door. Surely her job couldn't be in jeopardy on
the strength of this morning? Surely it wasn't all over before it had even started?

CHAPTER TWO

'Hi Mum!' Alex gave Fleur a worried smile as he ran towards her. 'How did it go?'

'It was fine.'

'Honestly?'

Fleur nodded assuredly. Some things a seven-year-old didn't need to hear. 'Where's Ben?'

'He's in time-out—he had to stay behind for talking too much. He shouldn't be long.'

As if on cue, Ben appeared, smiling happily, not remotely fazed by his short time in the sin bin. Fleur tried to ignore the unsettling contrast between the two boys. Alex would have been completely devastated—everything these days seemed to unnerve him. Not, of course, that she wanted him to be naughty at school, but he did need to relax a bit more. Kathy was probably right. The extra time with Ben would help, and maybe some of Ben's happy-go-lucky nature would rub off on Alex. Once again it was rammed home to Fleur that she needed this job for so much more than the money.

By the time Kathy arrived the kids had devoured a bowl of potato chips and a drink and were finishing up their homework.

'You're kidding.' Kathy laughed as she saw the boys with their heads down at the dining room table. 'I usually have to resort to blackmail. I hear you did a great job this morning.'

'From who?' Fleur asked doubtfully.

'Oh, just the general buzz around the place. How good it is to have you back, that sort of thing.'

'Fancy a cuppa?'

Kathy shook her head. 'Better not. Ben...' she called, picking up his school bag before giving Fleur a wicked grin. 'What did you think of the Italian stallion? And don't try and tell me you didn't notice him—I simply won't believe you. Apparently he lost his temper with Danny this afternoon,' she went on. 'Unfortunately I was stuck in Theatre or I'd have had a glass up to Danny's wall, but Beryl got the gist. He was roaring his head off about lack of *comunicazione* and team spirit and *disastros* waiting to happen. Something must have got under that gorgeous olive skin of his. He's been all moody and brooding this afternoon. Though it just made him all the sexier if you ask me. *Ben!*'

Waving cheerfully, Kathy dragged a reluctant Ben down the garden path. Fleur waved back, a sinking feeling of dread in her stomach. So she hadn't been imagining his mood after all. Mario Ruffini really was cross with her.

Dinner was simple, a shared omelette and salad on the veranda, with Alex carefully picking out anything green, but as she cleared the plates and made her way across the decking Alex's voice stopped Fleur in her tracks. 'Was it scary, Mum, going back?'

Battling the urge to force a smile and say 'of course not', Fleur turned slowly.

'A bit,' she admitted. 'How do you feel about it?'

Alex fiddled with the newspaper lying on the table in front of him. 'It'll be good going to Ben's and having him come here.' He paused. 'But...'

He didn't have to say it, the poor little guy. After all, the last time his mum had gone to work their lives had been thrown into turmoil. Fleur sat beside Alex and pulled him towards her, kissing the top of his blond curls as she waited for him to vocalise his fears. But even a mum, however devoted, doesn't always know what's going on in that little brain.

'I'm scared it's too much for you, Mum—being back there, I mean. You don't have to do it if you don't want to. I don't care if we don't go to see Movie World and everything.'

So he wasn't scared for himself, just for his mum. Holding him against her, Fleur thought her heart would burst with pride and love. Overnight her little boy had become a man. 'But a holiday in Queensland with a trip to Movie World would be nice, huh?'

Alex shrugged. 'I guess.'

'And a new game for your computer? Look, Alex, we're hardly going to starve if I don't go back to work—your dad made sure we were well looked after. We've got a beautiful home and a nice lifestyle, and money put aside for you to go to a nice high school, but all the little extras add up. I'm so proud of you for saying that it doesn't matter, but it *does* matter, darling, to me. And leaving aside the money, I'm a nurse, Alex. I used to love my work and I really missed it. This is going to make a big difference for both of us.'

Alex looked up. 'But—'

'I'm fine,' Fleur said firmly. And this time there was no question of forcing a smile, it came naturally. 'I've got friends there, good ones. If I get upset they'll help me through, that's what friends do. And at the end of the day I come home to you, so what have I got to worry about?'

Not just a man, every bit a male, Fleur thought ruefully as Alex picked up the paper and turned straight to the sports page.

'Just think, Mum, now you're working we'll be able to go to the footy lots!'

Now, there *was* a good reason to stay home!

Alex was bathed and in his pyjamas by seven, asking to watch a soap that was due to start.

'Everyone watches it, Mum. They all talk about it at school every morning and I'm the only one who doesn't get to see it. There's a hostage on tonight, the police are going to raid the school!'

Which was precisely why she didn't want him to watch it, but for once Fleur relented. 'Well, if you get nightmares tonight, don't come creeping into my bed.'

He didn't come creeping in, not that Fleur would have noticed anyway. As soon as her head hit the pillow it seemed the alarm clock rang, heralding yet another day.

Assigned to the cubicles in Section B, Fleur found herself awaiting Mario Ruffini's arrival with some trepidation. Determined to make at least a good second impression, she ensured that the minor injuries that frequented Section B were, as far as possible, ready to be seen by a doctor, removing home-made dressings, cleaning wounds and doing the occasional set of obs.

'Good morning, Sister.'

'Good morning, Mr Ruffini. The intern is in cubicle 3, seeing a sprained ankle, I've got a couple of minor hand injuries in cubicles one and two and a case of gastro down the end in cubicle seven.'

He nodded politely but didn't comment as he had a quick flick through the histories. Finally, he spoke. 'Nothing that can't wait for five minutes. I'm going to grab a coffee. How do you take yours?'

'Er, no, I'm fine, thanks.' Since when did the senior medical staff make the nurses coffee?

'Fine.'

Things obviously weren't fine. He'd been polite, he'd even offered to make her a drink, but Fleur just knew he was less than impressed with her.

He returned with a steaming mug, which he placed on a worktop before proceeding to see the patients.

Mario Ruffini *was* a good doctor, Fleur reluctantly decided. She'd wanted to be able to fault him, to find some flaw that his adoring fans had missed. But he was skilled in his assessments, polite and friendly to the patients and also incredibly fast. His only fault, if you could call it that, was the fact he obviously didn't like Fleur.

'I'm pretty sure the child in seven is early appendicitis. I've asked Wendy Edwards, the surgical registrar, to come down for a consult.'

'OK. I was actually just coming to find you. Felicity just buzzed from Resus—there's a patient in VT.'

VT was the abbreviation for ventricular tachycardia, a rapid but regular heartbeat that quickly exhausted a person and could soon lead to cardiac arrest.

Without comment, Mario picked up his stethoscope and made his way down the corridor.

The second he was gone the tension dissolved but, instead of feeling relaxed, Fleur felt curiously let down, deflated. Why she wanted Mario Ruffini's approval she wasn't sure, but bandaging a few sprained wrists and giving out a couple of tetanus shots were hardly the stuff to make him realise what a great nurse she was, Fleur mused, angrily restocking the stainless-steel trolleys.

'Didn't Danny sweep for land-mines this morning?' Wendy Edwards broke into her thoughts.

'Oh, hi, Wendy.'

'Fleur, it is you! It's so good to see you back. How are things?'

'Great,' Fleur lied easily. 'What's this about land-mines?'

'One's just gone off in Resus.' She grinned at Fleur's bemused expression. 'Our resident volcano, Mario Ruffini, just exploded. Don't tell me you haven't seen him in action yet.'

Fleur gave an embarrassed laugh. 'Actually, I have, about an hour into my first shift back. He hasn't gone off again, has he?'

'Big time.' Wendy pulled a face. 'I was tempted to stick my head in but I'm sure Felicity doesn't need an audience. Where's this kid he wants me to see?'

'Cubicle seven.' Fleur chewed anxiously on her lip. 'Do you know what it's about?'

'No,' Wendy said cheerfully. 'But you can fill me in when you find out.'

A quick look down the corridor confirmed that as usual Danny was nowhere to be seen, and the rest of the staff were either tied up or deliberately looking busy. Informing Lucy that she wouldn't be long, Fleur made her way to Resus.

As she opened the door a rocket didn't actually whiz past her ear, but there were definitely fireworks in the air.

'Great,' Mario shouted as she slipped in. 'Now they send in the nurse that "doesn't do Resus".'

'As opposed to what?' Fleur looked over to where Felicity stood, red-eyed, by the defibrillator. The drug trolley was in chaos, boxes and vials of drugs scattered over the top.

'As opposed to the nurse who doesn't know how basic equipment works, or where the drugs are kept.'

Fleur looked at the monitor. The patient was still in rapid VT.

'I want to cardiovert him, Felicity was trying to defibrillate him.'

'How many joules do you want?'

'Two hundred,' he snarled as Fleur flicked the switch necessary for cardioversion as opposed to defibrillation. Picking up the paddles, she applied them to the gel pads already in place on the patient's chest.

'Clear,' she called.

Mario briefly dropped the ambu-bag he was using to oxygenate the patient. As the patient's rhythm settled the doors flew open as the cardiac arrest team breathlessly arrived.

'Did you stop at the canteen on the way?' Mario shouted as they gathered around the patient's trolley. 'I assume you learnt in medical school that brain death occurs after three minutes.'

Charming, Fleur thought, her mouth set in a thin line as she assisted Felicity. At least his arrogance wasn't only for her benefit.

Danny, of course, turned up when all the drama was over. 'Fleur, you're in here!'

'Again!' Fleur said pointedly. 'Could I have a word, Danny?'

Danny's office was a mess—papers everywhere, overflowing trays of work. Taking a seat, she got straight to the point.

'Felicity didn't know how to set the machine for cardioversion.'

Danny let out a long sigh. 'Well, she should, she's been to enough lectures. I'll have a word.'

'I think a bit more that a word from you is needed, Danny. What is she doing in there when she doesn't know the equipment? And from what I can make out, she wasn't particularly crash hot on locating where the drugs and everything were kept. Mario Ruffini was furious and, as much as I don't approve of his methods, he had every right to be angry. She shouldn't be in there without supervision until she's more capable.'

'So what do you suggest?' He tossed the roster sheet across the table. 'Have a look at the choices, Fleur, and tell me who you'd put in there.'

Fleur ran her eyes down the names on the list. He had a fair point—there certainly wasn't a wealth of knowledge behind the names there.

'I've got a permanent advertisement for staff in the newspapers, I've got our department on every nursing agency's list and yet I still can't get any more experienced staff. I'm not trying to lay a guilt trip on you, Fleur. I took you on, knowing you weren't ready to go in there yet, and I'm prepared to wait. I don't want you to lose your confidence too early and leave, then we really will have achieved nothing. And as for Mario letting off steam, it's no big deal—he does it every day.'

'That doesn't make it all right!'

But Danny just laughed. 'He takes a bit of getting used to, I admit that, but he does grow on you in the end.'

'So do warts,' Fleur quipped. 'He shouldn't be allowed to jackboot his way around the department.' She paused for a moment before continuing. She'd known Danny a long time and they were friends, but it was still a rather hesitant Fleur that steered the conversation. 'How come you're not out there a bit more, Danny?'

'Someone's got to run the place.' He gestured to the desk around him. 'The fairies don't come in at night.'

'That never stopped you before. You were always out there helping out.'

'I'll have a word with Felicity,' he said, effectively ending the discussion. 'And I'll tell Mario to go a bit easy on her. Anyway, he's off for the rest of the week at some medical conference so you don't have to worry about him for a while.'

Fleur stood up. 'Speak to Felicity, but as for Mario I'd like to deal with him myself.'

Danny looked up to where she stood by the door. 'It might come better from you, given that you were there. Are you sure you don't mind?'

'I don't mind at all,' Fleur said darkly. 'In fact, it will be my pleasure.'

Infuriatingly, now she was actually ready for a confrontation Mario was nowhere in sight. After checking the cubicles and Resus, Fleur thought she'd try her luck in the obs ward. He wasn't there, of course, but the rather raucous laughter coming from the staffroom soon ended her search.

How did he do it? The doctors he'd been shouting at only fifteen minutes ago were now sharing a coffee and a joke with him, even Felicity had forgiven him and was joining in the laughter.

'Mr Ruffini?' Every eye turned to her as she stood primly in the doorway. 'I'd like a word, please.'

'Sure,' he said amicably, though not moving an inch. 'How can I help you?'

'Perhaps this might be better done in private.' Her voice left no room for doubt that she wasn't happy. Not remotely fazed, Mario gave a nonchalant shrug as he replaced his mug on the table.

'Excuse me, guys, I think I am being summoned.' He followed Fleur out of the room. 'Would my office be private enough for you, Sister?'

She gave a small nod of approval and followed him the short distance.

The sight of his office took the wind out of her sails.

Danny's was a mess but this was an absolute bombsite! Open-mouthed, she stared at the mountains of paper, the opened books, numerous coffee-cups.

'You wanted to speak with me?'

Dragging her eyes from his desk, Fleur remembered why she was here.

'I do. You may also have noticed that I asked to speak with you in private.'

'Yes.' He gave her a quizzical look, before his face broke into a grin. 'Do you want me to check for bugs?'

'Don't be so flippant!' Fleur checked herself instantly. This was a consultant she was talking to after all, not Alex—though his office did somehow resemble her son's bedroom when left unchecked!

'The reason I asked to speak to you in private is because I believe that when someone has a grievance, while I agree it should be aired, there is a correct way of going about it.'

'I am sorry, Sister, I really don't understand what you are talking about.' He gestured to his chair. 'May I sit for this?'

His question was unnecessary and curiously insolent, and Fleur stood rigid as he calmly made his way around the desk.

'You screaming at the staff in Resus is not only rude, it is ineffective. In the time you spent shouting at Felicity you could have shown her how to work the machine. I don't know how they do it in Italy, but it certainly doesn't wash here.'

'Doesn't wash?' He screwed up his forehead.

'You know exactly what I mean.'

'No, Sister, I don't. In fact, since you bring it up, I will tell you how things are done in Italy. The staff there are qualified and competent. I do not have to ask three times for a drug, I do not have to stop bagging an unconscious patient and deprive them of oxygen so that I can show the nurse how the machine works. Now do you understand why I shout? And contrary to what you say, I happen to find my methods extremely effective. I got the drug, didn't I? I got a nurse who could operate the equipment!'

'There are better ways of going about things,' Fleur said, though with rather less conviction.

'On that we can agree.' He gave her a smile but it did little to reassure her—Mario had definitely not finished proving his point! 'For example, a better way might be to have the associate charge nurse, which I've been told you are, in Resus instead of down in Section B, doing the stuff that is taught to Girl Guides. Who knows? If the nurse unit manager put in an occasional appearance now and then, we might even have a semblance of a well-run emergency department.'

'You don't know all the circumstances,' Fleur replied hotly.

'So enlighten me.'

She was good and mad now and in no position to pour out her heart to this insufferable man. Turning smartly on her heel, she wrenched the door open.

'Running off again, Sister? You really don't like to be where the action is, do you?'

Fleur turned, her eyes blazing. 'After hearing so many reports about how wonderful you were, Mr Ruffini, I thought we might be able to discuss this. I was obviously wrong. But as you yourself pointed out, I *am* an associate charge nurse, so next time you have a problem with one of my staff, please, have the common courtesy to allow me to deal with it before you lose your temper.'

'I don't doubt that there will be a next time, but I will certainly bear it in mind. Oh, and, Sister?'

Her hand tightened on the doorhandle but she forced herself to answer evenly. 'Yes, Mr Ruffini.'

'Would you mind fetching my coffee? I think I left it in the staffroom.'

She didn't slam the door, that would have been childless and pointless. She didn't even come up with a smart reply. But the salt cellar was so achingly close to his mug on the coffee-table and she was so blinded with unvented fury that Fleur did what was probably the one reckless thing she had ever done in her life.

And that was that.

War had been declared.

CHAPTER THREE

FLEUR let out an involuntary cry of anguish as she watched Alex leap to grab the football, only to be knocked sideways to the ground by the opposing team. Resisting the urge to run onto the footy pitch, she stood there nervously chewing on her bottom lip as Alex picked himself up, covered in mud but apparently none the worse for wear. Casting an anxious look in his mother's direction, he gave her a thumbs-up sign before joining his team-mates in yet another mad dash for the oval ball.

'The more I see of the game, the less I understand.' A deep, heavily accented voice that could only belong to one person broke her concentration. Blushing furiously, Fleur gave a small nod of agreement. What on earth was Mario Ruffini doing at Auskick?

'They call it football, and yet they handball, run with the ball, throw the ball. It isn't even a proper football—it looks like a rugby ball to me. And it's such a rough game.'

'You're not wrong there,' Fleur muttered, wishing he would be quiet so she could pay attention to the game or, more to the point, Alex.

'In my country we play real football, or soccer as you call it here. Now, *that* I understand. But I am slowly starting to learn this game of yours.' He spoke as if Australian Rules football was a game she'd invented personally. 'I brought my nephew along today, he loves it with a passion. I'm hoping to get to see a few real matches while I'm here. You know, follow it properly.'

Fleur shrugged, staring pointedly ahead. 'Oh, well, when in Rome and all that.'

'Not for a while yet. I'm here for a year.'

'Pardon?' Turning for the first time, she was somewhat taken back when she saw Mario. Out of a suit and dressed in black jeans and black crew-neck jumper, he was definitely worth a second look! Sporting a heavy few days of growth on his chin and his dark hair for once unkempt, Mario looked rather more Mexican than Italian. As if he should be in a dusty bar, drinking tequila with a bandanna on his head, not standing in the middle of a muddy footy field in the bayside suburbs of Melbourne.

'You asked me when I went back to Rome. I was explaining I was in Australia for a year.'

Fleur gave him a bemused look. 'Oh, no.' She laughed as she realised what had happened. 'I meant, when in Rome, do as the Romans do. It's a proverb.'

It was his turn to look bemused. 'A proverb—what is this proverb?'

Fleur thought for a moment 'It's like a saying,' she said slowly. 'An adage. When in Australia, do as the Australians do.' From the lost expression on his face he obviously didn't understand. 'You've no idea what I'm talking about, have you? When in France, do as the French do. Like…' She tried to conjure up an image. 'Drink red wine and eat lots of cheese and look fabulous.'

A slow smile crept across his face. 'So when in Australia, I watch footy and have barbecues and drink cold beer?'

'That's about it.'

'Thank you for explaining this to me.'

Glad that at least had been cleared up, Fleur turned back to the game, trying to concentrate while achingly aware of his presence. Cringing as she recalled her actions earlier in the week, she'd expected him to either ignore her or at least treat her in the same curt fashion he did at work, but Mario seemed intent on being friendly as he hovered next to her.

'Of course you can apply it to smaller things,' Fleur said, surprising herself by resurrecting the conversation. 'It doesn't just have to be about countries.'

'Now I really am confused.'

'Well, say you came to my house and you smoked. I don't smoke, so I'd hope you'd respect that and not smoke in my house.'

'But I don't smoke.'

How had she got into this? 'No. But it if you did, as you put your cigarettes back in your pocket you might say, sadly perhaps, "Oh, well, when in Rome." Look, I'm sorry. I probably haven't explained myself very well.'

But Mario's blue eyes were smiling now as realisation dawned. 'No, I think you have explained things very well. Thank you.'

For a moment they turned back to the game but he was obviously intent on chatting. 'See, there is my nephew Ricky.' He pointed to a dark-haired boy sporting the red and black colours of the Essendon football team. Fleur actually knew Ricky, to look at anyway. He was in the same class as Alex. 'He is the main reason I am in this country. My sister Teresa emigrated some years ago. It's hard, realising you've got a nephew on the other side of the world that, apart from a few phone calls and pictures, you don't even know. When the chance for this job came up I jumped at it.'

'Do you live at your sister's?' Fleur asked.

'Of course. Why wouldn't I?'

Fleur shrugged. Mario looked more the penthouse type. 'Doesn't it cramp your style a bit?'

He laughed loudly. 'Teresa is not my mother, thank goodness. You realise, if my mother saw us talking like this she would be booking the church already?'

'That bad, huh?'

Mario nodded. 'Another reason that I am here—a year off from blind dates was an added incentive. Anyway, the purpose of my year here is to catch up with my sister and get to know my nephew, so living with Teresa makes sense. Which is your son?'

'Alex, the one in the helmet.' He was easy to point out as Alex was the only child wearing the non-compulsory protective headgear.

'Has he a head injury?'

Fleur gritted her teeth. Mario might be good-looking but he definitely talked too much. 'No, that's what I'm trying to prevent.'

'Oh.'

His single word spoke volumes. So maybe she was a bit over-protective, but she was sick of having to justify herself for being a responsible parent. 'I'm sure that if the other parents realised the dangers, every child on this field would be wearing a helmet.'

Mario didn't look convinced. 'I see your son wears the yellow and black colours. That means he supports the Richmond Tigers, yes?'

'Yes.'

'They are my adopted team, too. And do you take him to the matches?'

Fleur shook her head. 'No, well, at least not if I can help it. This is bad enough.'

Mario laughed. 'So you're not into football. Well, I guess that's what fathers were invented for.'

His comment was well meant, of course, but Fleur had to bite her lip as the sharp sting of tears reached her eyes.

Thankfully the whistle blew and she was saved from any further conversation as three excited little boys ran in their direction.

'I kicked a goal, Mum. Did you see?' Alex, bright eyed and breathless from exertion, ripped off his much-hated headgear and started to cough.

'Yes, I saw. You played really well.' Scrabbling in her bag, she pulled out his Ventolin inhaler but Alex pushed it away.

'Mum, I'm fine.'

'You're coughing, you know how it starts.'

'But I've been running for an hour. I'm fine, honest. Hey, Ricky,' he said turning to his team-mate. 'Did you see me kick a goal?'

Putting the inhaler back into her bag, Fleur was aware that Mario was watching her. 'I'd best get them home.'

'You have two children? I didn't realise.'

'No, just the one. Ben here belongs to my friend Kathy—you'd know her from Accident and Emergency— Kathy Fisk.'

'I know Kathy, good for a gossip.'

Fleur grinned. 'That's the one.'

'Well, I'll see you tomorrow, Fleur. Are you working then?'

Fleur nodded. 'How was your conference?'

'Interesting, but now I suffer for the time away from the department. I am going to drop Ricky off and then head in to work. Who knows? I might even get a chance to clear my desk.'

Fleur doubted that. A bulldozer was the only thing that would clear a space in that office. 'Well, I hope it's quiet for you. See you, Mr Ruffini.'

'I'll catch you later. Isn't that what they say here?' And

taking Ricky by his muddy hand, they headed off to the car park.

Walking home, Fleur tried to keep one ear on the boys' conversation as her mind kept drifting back to her chance meeting with Mario. Out of work he'd seemed so much more friendly, amenable even, nothing like the volatile autocrat she'd witnessed before. And Kathy had been right. He really was gorgeous... 'Ricky's dad's taking him to the footy on Saturday.' Alex announced.

'Mine, too,' Ben said proudly.

If only Greg, Kathy's husband, supported the same team as Alex, Fleur thought for the hundredth time. It wasn't that Greg minded taking Alex to the footy—in fact, he'd offered umpteen times—but Alex was his father's son and had no interest in the other teams. Unless the Tigers were playing he simply didn't want to know. She did take him now and then—usually when Alex had nagged long and effectively and Fleur was on one of her guilt trips about Alex missing out on a father figure—but it was a very occasional treat. The only pleasure Fleur got out of the Tigers winning was seeing Alex's face, but even that prize came at a price—an extra load of washing so that Alex could wear his beloved footy jumper to school on the Monday. A 'treat' dreamt up by the school principal, who obviously didn't have to scrape off the mud and steam-iron the blessed thing at seven-thirty on a Monday morning.

Kathy, as always, had just put the kettle on. 'Thanks so much.' She grinned as Fleur flattened herself against the wall to avoid the two young boys jostling past. 'It's my turn for the torture chamber next week.'

Luckily Kathy hated footy as much as she did and didn't even bother to ask how the morning had gone. Sunday mornings had become fondly known between them as 'job share' long before Fleur's return to work. It suited them both well. Greg was a long-distance truck driver who more often than not worked weekends, and as for Alex's dad...well, he would have loved the 'job' but fate had put a cruel end to that.

'We nearly didn't make it this morning,' Fleur admitted. 'Alex practically refused to put his helmet on. I told him that unless he wears it he simply isn't going, so don't take any nonsense from him next week. If he starts to play up, ring me on your mobile and I'll come and fetch him. He's got to realise I mean what I say. It's for his own good.'

'Is it?' Kathy knew she was on dangerous ground here but she persisted, trying to ignore the pursed lips in Fleur's pale face. 'Do you really think it's good for him to be the only kid out there padded to the hilt?'

'It's a rough game.' Fleur said tartly.

'And Alex is a boy. Rough games are the ones they play best. Look, I know it might be none of my business, but you're my best friend so I'm making it my business. You know how mean kids can be sometimes about the tiniest thing? Alex wearing that headgear makes him stand out, makes him a target. Not to mention you rushing over every five minutes and driving past the playground umpteen times a day while he's at school.'

'I do not,' Fleur said hotly. 'I mean, if I'm going past on the way to the shops I might slow down—'

'And nearly cause a pile-up behind you as you crane your neck, trying to see if Alex is playing with anyone—'

'I know, I know,' Fleur interrupted. 'Look, Kathy, in every other way I've got my life together. I'm independent, I've got great friends and a bit of a social life under way.' Kathy's sceptical look deserved an answer. 'Or at least I'm starting to—it's just hard, leaving Alex. I know I'm over-protective, and I am trying to let go, I really am. I just feel so responsible, if anything were to happen to him, I mean. When Rory was alive, there was someone to share it with…' Her voice trailed off.

'I'm sorry, Fleur. Maybe I shouldn't have said anything. I know it's hard for you and you're doing wonderfully.'

'I wish I believed that.'

'But you are,' Kathy said emphatically. 'You're a wonderful mother. Alex is a great kid.'

'But he's not happy, Kathy. He's struggling to make friends, he's even started to wet the bed again. I know my anxiety translates to him but I just can't seem to help myself.'

'You *are* helping yourself, Fleur. You're back at work, getting on with your life. Alex is going to be just fine, if only you let him.'

'The only trouble with that,' Fleur said slowly, 'is that it's so much easier said than done.'

'Ricky's eight next month. He's having a sleep-over party.'

Hearing the wistful note in his voice Fleur trod carefully. 'That sounds nice.'

'He hasn't given out his invitations yet. I expect Ben will be going—he gets invited to lots of parties.'

'You go to parties, too,' Fleur pointed out.

'But not like Ben.'

He was right, Fleur thought with a sigh as she cleared the plates and Alex's untouched vegetables. But Ben's father hadn't died two weeks before he'd started school. Kathy had been happy to get involved with the coffee mornings, school runs and the social chitchat at the school gates while she herself had stood there, shivering despite the hot summer sun, dark glasses covering her reddened eyes, too scared of breaking down to respond to the well-meaning offers of help.

Fleur thought back to Alex's last two birthday parties—low-key affairs with sombre relatives ducking out for a weep at every turn. Alex deserved a treat.

'Tell you what, this year why don't we do something special for your birthday? How about a tenpin bowling party?'

Alex's eyes widened. 'Really?'

'Well, now I'm working I reckon that you deserve a treat.'

'Cool! How many people can I invite?'

Fleur grinned. 'Alex, it's weeks away. I'm sure there's plenty of time to write up a list.'

The prospect of a party lifted Alex's mood sufficiently for him to put away the water jug and rather clumsily wipe down the table without being asked three times.

By the time Alex was finally asleep, all Fleur wanted to do was collapse in front of the television but, knowing it would make the early morning start impossible she set about making Alex's packed lunch for tomorrow and sorting out their school and nursing uniforms.

Satisfied she was organised for the morning, Fleur settled down on the sofa, determined not to brood on the events of the week, but brooding was obviously the theme tonight. Kathy's words had really rattled her. Fleur knew she exacerbated Alex's nervousness, knew she had to let up a bit, but it was so damned hard. Everything was so damned hard without Rory.

Time healed.

It didn't; it didn't.

Sure, she didn't wake up each morning sobbing like she used to. Didn't wonder how she'd get through the next hour, let alone the day. But the agony of her loss was with her with every inch of the way. And she was angry, too. Not just for her and for Alex, but for Rory. Angry for all he'd missed out on. For the roll of the dice that had taken him away from all that he'd loved.

Time didn't heal, Fleur decided.

You just learnt to live with the pain.

The ringing of the doorbell caught her unawares and it was a rather cautious Fleur that pulled the front door open, peering through the security door at her surprise visitor.

'Fleur, I must apologise for the lateness of the hour.'

'Mr Ruffini?'

'Mario, please. I know it is late, but what I have to say simply cannot wait for the morning.'

His English, though excellent, was somewhat broken and Fleur was sure she could detect a note of urgency. Unclipping the security door, she gestured for him to come through, her heart sinking as she did so.

Mario looked as stunning as ever and Fleur felt drab in comparison, dressed in a sloppy jumper and leggings. When he didn't break immediately into a speech about her earlier inefficiency, it was left to Fleur to break the rather awkward silence.

'How did you know where I lived?'

'Don't worry, the hospital didn't give out your address.' It was a strict work policy that the emergency book which held the staff's addresses and telephone numbers, in case of a change to the roster or a major influx of patients, was to be used only for what it was intended—emergencies. Too many lessons had been learnt in the past of the dangers of giving out such private information. 'I used simpler methods, or so I thought.'

Fleur gave him bemused look.

'The phone book,' he explained. 'There were only two F. Hadleys in the area, and Frank was very helpful.'

'Frank?' He'd really lost her now!

'The other F. Hadley thought I'd just come from the airport and was trying to track down a long lost relative. It's a long story,' he added, looking at her totally confused expression. 'The long and the short of it is that Frank and I are playing lawn bowls next Sunday.'

So he'd made another friend. 'Er, do you want a cup of coffee, or a beer perhaps?' Fleur asked, trying to think if there were any stubbies in the fridge.

'Coffee would be wonderful, but only one lump of salt, please.' Following her through to the kitchen, he watched in silence as Fleur filled two cups from the filter machine.

'It was an accident,' she blurted out finally.

'And do you always blush so much when you lie?'

Fleur handed him the cup. 'Always,' she admitted sheepishly.

Mario just laughed. 'You like a decent brew also?'

'I might even start drinking it at work now you've bought the machine.' If I've still got a job, she nearly added.

Taking the cup from her, their fingers brushed and Fleur suddenly felt incredibly awkward.

'May we sit?'

'Of course. Come through.'

The lounge was large and spacious, but a cricket field would have felt suffocating at the moment. 'Look, I know what this is about,' Fleur ventured. 'I'd like to apologise…'

Mario put up his hand, effectively halting her from going any further. 'It is I who should be apologising.'

'You?' Fleur asked, nonplussed. 'But why?'

'For my thoughtless comments this morning. I had no idea you were a widower.'

'A widow,' Fleur corrected gently. 'And, please, don't give it a moment's thought. You weren't to know.'

'Perhaps not, and I am grateful to you for accepting my apology. But that doesn't excuse this week's events.'

Here it came! Fleur braced herself for a few sharp words Italian-style but again the wind was taken from her sails when he continued, 'I most certainly should have known that you were a *widow*...' He learns quickly, Fleur thought. 'I am speechless, no, I am furious, that Danny did not have the decency to tell me. And not just me—all the staff should have been notified about the terrible circumstances surrounding your husband's death.'

'But most know anyway,' Fleur said, instantly defending Danny. 'I'm sure Danny just assumed—'

'Then he should not have. He goes on and on about team spirit, comradeship, and then when it really matters he just *assumes* things are taken care of. I only found out from a passing comment he made this afternoon. I have teared him off a strip.'

Fleur didn't bother to correct him as she was somewhat taken back by his obvious anger.

'This must have been a terrible week for you, and undoubtedly there will be many more to come. The staff should be sensitive, helping you through. How can we if we are not even told about something as important as this?'

Fleur let out a sigh of relief. From the way he was talking it sounded as if he expected her to come back. 'I *am* sorry, though, and not just about the coffee. I feel as if I've let everybody down.'

'No, Fleur, they have let *you* down. It all should have been handled so much better. Danny told me you were actually on duty when your husband was brought in.'

Fleur nodded simply.

'Are you able to tell me about it? Maybe then I can help.'

'I doubt it.' Looking up, she saw his eyes were fixed directly on her.

Embarrassed, nervous, her eyes flicked quickly away, her gaze coming to rest on her wedding picture. Perhaps she should tell him. Perhaps then he would understand her fear of going into Resus. And who knew? Maybe he *could* help.

Swallowing a couple of times, Fleur's voice came out quietly and Mario had to lean forward to catch what she was saying, his eyes never once leaving her face.

'It was just a normal Saturday night, busy as usual. I was down for Resus. We got an alert that a multiple MVA was coming in. A motor vehicle accident,' she explained unnecessarily, but Mario just nodded his understanding as she tentatively continued. 'As the news started to trickle in we learnt there was a stolen car involved. The police had been in pursuit, and one officer was trapped and one dead. I assured myself at first that Rory couldn't be in-volved—he was a detective, not out on patrol. Then the paramedic bringing in the first victim made a casual re-mark about it having been an unmarked police car. I started to panic then. I knew I had to call him. I knew that I would be useless for work until I heard for myself that he was safe...'

'Go on,' he urged, but gently. Making his way across the room, he sat beside her on the sofa as she struggled to continue, his hand reaching for hers.

'I hadn't even dialled the station number when I saw Danny walking towards me. His face was grim and I just knew what was coming. I can remember actually feeling sorry for Danny when he delivered the news. It must have been the worst moment in his nursing career—telling a close colleague that her husband, the father of her five-year-old son, was seriously injured, on his way in with full resuscitation in progress.'

'Did you have to work on your husband?'

'No, nothing so dramatic. We weren't so short-staffed then.' Fleur managed a wry laugh but there was a catch in it and she started to cry. 'I just sat in the staffroom with the nurse supervisor. She kept offering to make phone calls, but I needed to know how bad it was for myself before I tried to tell others.' She was crying in earnest now. 'Then Danny was in the doorway, with Kathy beside him. They didn't have to say anything. One look at their faces and I knew it was over.' She looked at the picture on the mantelpiece, the utter despair in her voice so achingly apparent that Mario wrapped his arm around her as if he could somehow shield her from the bitter end that was coming. 'I knew then that Rory, my Rory, Alex's dad, wasn't going to be coming home, not ever.'

He let her cry for a while, his arm tightly around her as she wept onto his chest. Finally, when her mascara had long since gone and she'd reached the hiccoughing stage, he gently sat her up. Without a word he made his way to the kitchen, returning with a glass of water which Fleur sipped gratefully.

'I'm sorry. I haven't cried like that for ages.'

Mario flicked his hand dismissively. 'Tears don't embarrass me.' He sat down again beside her. 'Tell me, Fleur, why did you come back, after all that you've been through? Surely if you need the money you could work on the wards, save yourself this heartache?'

'Believe me, I've thought about it. But I'm an emergency nurse, Mario. I even used to be a good one. The wards never really appealed to me but maybe it's worth thinking about. Maybe it is too soon to go back to Emergency. Look at the mess I made with Mrs Green.'

'But you were excellent.'

Fleur looked out from under the fringe where she was now hiding and flicked her hair back. 'Now I know that you're just being kind. I completely froze. I spoke to Danny about it. He said it understandable, given the circumstances, but I still feel terrible.'

Mario looked at her closely for what seemed an age, and as a blush started to spread across her cheeks, Fleur let her hair fall over her eyes again. Her fringe was a strangely comforting refuge from his steady gaze.

'When you found Mrs Green, what did you do?' Mario asked finally.

'I called for help,' Fleur answered quickly. 'You saw me.'

'No, Fleur, tell me from the moment you went over to her exactly what happened.'

'Well…' Fleur cast her mind back, not sure what he was getting at. 'I called her name a couple of times. When I realised she was unresponsive I checked her pulse and her airway.'

'Which was blocked, yes?'

Fleur nodded. 'One set of her teeth was hanging out and the other was obstructing her airway. So I cleared the obstruction, laid her flat, suctioned her airway, inserted an airway and administered some oxygen, and then I put her into the recovery position. Then I went to press the emergency button. You came in then.'

Mario nodded. 'And in that time did you freeze or panic? Did you compromise your patient's safety?'

'No,' Fleur said slowly, blinking a couple of times as realisation dawned. 'In fact, I didn't even think about

Rory—that was my husband—until we were in the resuscitation room. It was then that I froze.'

'No,' said Mario, again correcting her. 'It was not until she was safely in Resus and you had put out an emergency call and other staff were present that you naturally started to relax and think about your husband. But even then you stayed until Danny was present.'

'But you had to shout at me to get me to pull up the drug.'

Mario grinned. 'I shout a lot in there, and if you spend some time with me you'll learn not to take it to heart. Anyway you responded. You *did* pull up the drug. Never once was Mrs Green's safety put in danger. My argument is that, had I known, I could have made things a bit easier for you, or at least been aware that it was more than first-day jitters.'

Fleur hadn't thought of it like that, yet she still found it impossible to just forgive herself. 'Even so, maybe it is too soon to be back.'

'No!' His words were sharp. 'There will never be a perfect time, given what has happened to you. But if Emergency is where you want to be, and with the staff looking out for you, supporting you, you will be *magnifico*.'

Fleur grinned. 'A slight exaggeration, I think.'

'Not at all. You are far too hard on yourself. Are you a robot, a machine? No, you are a woman.' He gave her a slow grin. 'I apologise again—that might sound sexist with your strange laws here. You are a human being with feeling is what I am trying to say, and probably a better nurse, too, for the pain you have suffered. Don't let all that knowledge go to waste.

'Now, to show that I am sincere in my apology and to

extend the hand of friendship as I feel we got off to rather
a poor start, I would like to issue an invitation to you.'

Fleur opened the envelope he handed her with a sigh.
Surely not another grief counsellor's business card? She
could line the walls with them. It was almost as bad. 'Tickets to the football?'

'I was going to take my brother-in-law and nephew, but
they refused as their team is playing at Colonial Stadium.
I remembered that Alex likes the Richmond Tigers also,
and I wondered if you two might like to join me?'

Fleur shook her head firmly. 'It's very kind of you, but
football's really not my thing.'

'I understand that—you made it very clear this morning.
But if you would at least look at the tickets, you will see
they are for a corporate box. The company that has invited
me is having a family day and there will be other children
going. You will be wined and dined, you don't even have
to look at the game, and Alex will have the time of his
life, watching the footy.'

He pronounced it foot*ee* and Fleur found herself smiling.

'I really can't. People might talk…' She was scraping
the barrel for excuses now!

'Then let them talk! What would they say? I have already gone out with most of them already. I fully intend
to make the most of my year here and see everything this
city has to offer, and many of your colleagues have ac-
companied me on my sightseeing trips. Now, the MCG is,
I hear, the Mecca of sport for Melburnians. I simply cannot
miss it. If it makes you feel any better, Delorus and I are
going out on Friday to a restaurant in Chinatown, you and
me to the footy on Saturday and then Frank and I are
playing bowls on Sunday. So you see, it is all innocent.
We really won't set tongues wagging.'

Fleur laughed, thinking of Delorus telling the world about her 'date'. 'I wouldn't bet on it.'

'So you will come, please? It would make me feel better and Alex would enjoy it, no?'

'Yes.' Realising her mistake, Fleur hastily continued. 'I meant, what you should have said is that Alex will enjoy it, *yes.*'

'And you are going to join me?'

'No.'

But under that blue gaze her resolve was weakening.

He gave her the cheekiest of grins. 'What you should have said is that Alex will enjoy it so *yes.*'

Fleur knew when she was beaten. 'Your English is better than you make out, I think.' The tickets were hot in her hands, his eyes burning into her as he awaited her decision. 'All right, then, I'll come,' she said, watching as his grin widened. 'But I'm warning you, Mario, I really don't like the football!'

CHAPTER FOUR

FLEUR didn't deliberately not tell Kathy about Mario's invitation, but she most certainly didn't volunteer the information. Of course, though, once she'd told Alex and he in turn excitedly told the whole school and anyone else who happened to be passing, it was only a matter of time before a rather indignant Kathy demanded to know how come she was the last to know.

'Because it's no big deal,' Fleur said, calmly filling the kettle. 'He had some extra tickets and he knew Alex supported Richmond. Anyway, he felt awful for what he said at Auskick, though he had no reason to. That's all there is to it. I don't even want to go.'

'And you expect me to swallow that? Come on, Fleur, you must be at least a bit excited?'

'No.' Fleur answered truthfully—'terrified' would be a more apt description.

'Well, I would be. How long does a match go on for? Two hours, plus the half-time break, pre-match drinks and all that. That's three hours in the dashing Mario Ruffini's company.'

She meant well, Fleur reasoned, suddenly tempted to gag Kathy with the teatowel.

'What are you wearing?'

'Jeans, I guess.'

'Fleur!' Kathy sounded horrified. 'It's a corporate box you're going to. You've really got no idea, have you? You'll have to wear a suit.'

'To the football? I don't even own a suit, and I'm definitely not going to buy one.'

Famous last words. Picking Alex and Ben up at three-thirty, she rather guiltily stuffed her bulging carrier bags into the boot before she walked over to the school playground. A small fortune had been spent on the most gorgeous camel-coloured suit and the softest suede loafers, and then, when there had been no turning back, it had seemed rather pointless not to buy the cream camisole to wear underneath.

Bowling parties, extravagant suits, going back to work—it was costing her a small fortune. At this rate she'd be putting her hands up for extra shifts.

But it was worth it, Fleur admitted when she dressed on Saturday and stood in front of the mirror. For once her hair had behaved and hung in a straight blonde curtain, not a kink or frizz in sight—possibly thanks to the ridiculously expensive hair serum that had found its way into her shopping trolley.

'You look great, Mum. Is that new?'

'No,' Fleur lied, crossing her fingers as she did so. 'I just haven't worn it in ages. You don't look so bad yourself.' Wearing dark trousers and a smart blazer, he looked the image of his father and Fleur swallowed a lump in her throat. Alex didn't notice, instead screwing up his nose as he looked down at his attire.

'I'd rather be wearing my footy jumper,' he said for the hundredth time.

'Alex, we're going to a corporate box. Now, you remember what I said about behaving. No shouting—'

'OK, OK.' At the sound of a car pulling into the drive, Alex made a dash for the window. 'He's here. Nice car!'

Letting him in, Fleur brushed off Mario's extravagant compliments.

'Fleur, you look magnificent—*bella!*—and, Alex, you look so smart and handsome.'

'I wanted to wear my footy jumper but Mum said no.'

'I know,' Mario sighed dramatically. 'But look.' And lifting up his smart beige trousers, Fleur couldn't help but laugh out loud at the sight of his solid calves encased in yellow and black footy socks.

Alex was won over in an instant. 'Cool! Mum, can I go and put mine on?'

'Well, hurry, then.'

As he scampered off Mario laughed. 'He loves his team.'

Fleur nodded. 'How come you don't go for Essendon like the rest of your family?'

'What would we fight over at the dinner table?'

Despite all her protestations about hating football, in the sumptuous warmth of a corporate box with an endless supply of delicate finger food in one hand and a glass of a delicious fruity Australian red in the other, to Fleur's utter surprise she felt herself start to relax and enjoy herself. And all this before the starting whistle had even been blown!

Australian Rules football was taken very seriously in Victoria. It was followed devotedly by all and the weekend's games were discussed in depth on the following Monday. Tuesday and Wednesday, too, come to that. Of course, there was the occasional oddball like Fleur, for whom it held absolutely no charm, but for today at least it had an extra fan. Her nerves at spending so much time with Mario soon vanished as they mingled and chatted with the twenty-five or so other guests.

'Mum, they're doing a sweepstake—five dollars each.' Alex held his hand out excitedly.

'You're too young to bet,' Fleur pointed out. 'But I suppose I can put a bet on for you.'

'You have to have a bet, too,' Mario insisted. 'I say Tigers by twelve points.'

Fishing in her purse, Fleur pulled out a ten-dollar note. 'Who are they playing?'

Mario looked at her, aghast. 'You mean you don't even know? It's the Sydney Swans.'

Fleur gave him a defiant look 'Well, then, the Swans by ten points.'

Shaking his head Mario wrote down her prediction. 'And what about you young man?'

'Tigers by fifty points.'

Fleur handed over her money. 'Well, I can kiss that goodbye.'

It was a good game, Fleur grudgingly admitted afterwards. In fact, it was a *great* game. Despite her earlier warnings to Alex to sit and behave, when the Richmond Tigers had surged ahead in the final quarter and kicked five goals straight at six points apiece, the whole corporate box, Fleur included, had erupted into a fury of excited cheers and yells. The final siren had heralded a fifty-six-point win and it had been Alex who'd screamed the loudest when, as the person with the closest prediction, he'd won the sweepstake.

'I've won one hundred and twenty-five dollars!' Rushing over to his new-found friends, they all started to work out just what Alex could do with his new-found fortune.

Mario looked over at Fleur and smiled warmly. 'He's had a great day.'

'Thanks to you. There haven't been too many of them lately.'

Leaning over, he topped up her wineglass. 'It must have been tough on him.'

Fleur nodded. 'He keeps it all in, but I know he's hurting.'

'Is he seeing anyone?'

'No, he did at first. He used to go to a counsellor once a week, but it seemed to make things worse. I thought that he'd started to pick up a bit, but recently he's seemed to be going backwards.'

'In what way?'

Fleur hesitated before continuing. Kathy was really the only person she really discussed this sort of thing with, but under Mario's steady gaze she found herself starting to confide, to loosen up and share her concerns.

'Well, he's so anxious—about everything. He's not making many friends—you know, on his own at playtime, not asked to parties, that sort of thing.'

'Doesn't Ben play with him?'

'A bit, but generally he's off with his own little gang.'

'Ricky's having a party soon. I'm sure he can ask Alex along without making it a big deal.'

Fleur shook her head. 'No, please, don't. I hear Ricky's having a sleep-over. Alex can't go to one of those.'

Mario's forehead creased. 'Teresa, my sister, is very responsible—'

'I'm sure she is,' Fleur interrupted quickly. 'It's just that Alex…well, he wets the bed.'

'Since his father died?' Mario's voice was very gentle and Fleur felt her shoulders, which had automatically stiffened as she'd told him, suddenly relax.

'Well, it started then, but he did become dry about six months ago. He was doing so well, but in the last week or two it's flared up again. I think it might be due to me going back to work.'

'What does his GP say?'

'I haven't taken him yet,' Fleur admitted. 'Like I said,

it's only just started again and I was rather hoping it was just a relapse. My GP's on holiday for a couple of weeks and I didn't want to take him to a locum.'

'Fair enough,' Mario said. 'But before you put it down to anxiety you have to rule out the basics. Drop a fresh urine specimen in tomorrow to the lab—I'll leave a slip with them.'

'But you're off this weekend, and he's not complaining of any stinging or anything like that.'

'Doesn't mean that he hasn't got an infection. It's no big deal. I can drop off the slip first thing tomorrow, and then by Monday or Tuesday at the latest we'll have the results. If it is an infection we'd better get onto it straight away. If not, we can take it from there.'

He was right, of course, and Fleur gratefully nodded. 'Thanks again. I'd better round up Alex.' She made to stand up but Mario put out his hand, gently brushing her arm as he did so.

'I hope you weren't planning to leave before the scones and cream.'

Fleur groaned. 'Not more food. I honestly couldn't eat another thing.' But as Mario spooned generous amounts of strawberry jam and thick dollops of cream on the warm scones, Fleur weakened. 'Well, maybe just one.'

'I told you you didn't need to enjoy football to come here.'

'You realise, don't you, that all this spoiling is going to make it even harder for me to stand out there in the stands next time Alex begs me to go to the football?'

'In that case, I'll have to try and rustle up more tickets.' It was a casual remark, hardly meriting another thought. So why, then, wondered Fleur as they walked through the muddy car park, was she behaving like Alex and trying to work out how many matches were left in the footy season?

Why did she want to grab Mario's arm like a spoilt seven-year-old and ask *When?*

Even the ride home was fun, with Mario hanging his footy scarf out of the window so it trailed behind them as they drove along, prompting other Richmond fans to hoot their approval as they passed them. Fleur leant back against the soft leather seats, turning slightly so she could answer Alex's never-ending stream of questions from the back seat. The angle allowed her more than a glimpse of Mario, and Fleur drank it all in—the strong features, the long straight nose, thick dark eyebrows and even thicker eyelashes. Her eyes flicked down to his hands. Beautiful hands, she found herself thinking. Veins thick beneath the olive skin, white neat nails, a heavy gold bracelet around his wrist. Normally Fleur didn't like jewellery on a man, but this suited Mario. A flash of extravagance on him seemed somehow fitting.

As the car pulled up in her drive and Mario said his goodbyes to Alex, Fleur was suddenly hit with a longing for the day not to end.

'Do you want to come in for a coffee?' Her voice was casual but she found herself holding her breath as she awaited his answer.

'A coffee would be perfect.'

'I can show you my footy stickers.' Alex's eager voice chimed in.

'That would be great.'

Fleur couldn't help but feel disappointed that Mario greeted the prospect of the footy album with the same enthusiasm as her invitation for coffee. She left them to it, the two of them poring over various sports stars as she tackled the filter machine. The wine was definitely catching up with her, Fleur realised when she saw clear water gushing into the glass jar. Hastily she put a few generous scoops of coffee into the filter. Even filling the sugar bowl was an event in itself. What on earth's the matter with me? Fleur scolded herself as she wiped up a sticky mess of sugar from the kitchen bench.

'Smells good.' Mario joined her in the kitchen with a yawning Alex by her side.

'I'm tired, Mum.'

Fleur thought for a moment she was hearing things. Alex could be asleep on his feet and insist he was fine. 'I think I might go to bed.'

'But it's only seven o'clock.' Fleur protested, butterflies suddenly appearing as she realised her only ally was about to abandon her.

Mario ruffled the small boy's hair. 'It's been a pretty exciting day, hasn't it? I'm worn out, too.'

Alex nodded. 'Thanks for taking me, Mario. It's been great. I can't wait for Monday to tell all the kids at school.' He gave Fleur a kiss. ''Night, Mum.'

''Night, darling. I'll come and tuck you in in a moment.'

Never had making a simple cup of coffee seemed so complicated. She could feel his eyes on her as she poured the brew into the two cups and went through the milk and sugar routine. 'I should have some biscuits here some-where—if Alex hasn't swiped them,' she mumbled. All that was left were some green iced dinosaur shapes but such were her nerves at suddenly finding herself alone with him that Fleur hardly noticed as she arranged them on a plate. 'How was your night out with Delorus?'

'Even more exhausting than today. I don't know where she gets her energy. I'll be a wreck by Monday.'

Fleur laughed, thinking of Delorus's HRT comment. 'The weekend's still young yet.'

'Is it?' His deep voice stopped Fleur in mid-laugh. For a fraction of a second she caught his eye and there was definitely a frisson of something dangerous and exciting in the look that passed between them.

'I mean, you've got bowling with Frank Hadley tomorrow,' she said quickly, grabbing a biscuit from the plate and taking a hasty bite.

'Ah, yes, I forgot.' His face was suddenly a picture of concern as Fleur grimaced. He was over the room in a second. 'Fleur, are you all right? Did something I say upset you again?'

Looking up at his anxious face, Fleur let out a gurgle of laughter. 'No, it's not you. Just these revolting biscuits. There's so much sugar and colouring in them I'll probably be up all night. I can't believe I just ate one, let alone offered them to a guest.'

Their laughter broke the tension and they chatted easily for the next half-hour or so about work, the hospital, Mario's family in Rome. She found him fascinating, a wonderful story-teller, his not quite perfect English making for the odd hilarious mistake, his expressive hands gesturing as he wildly exaggerated. Only when he stood up to go, when he said goodnight and made his way to the front door did the tension return. Turning, he took her shoulders in his hands and moved his face towards her, kissing her first on her right cheek and then on her left. Fleur stood there dumbly, not offering her cheeks as she knew she should, the casual European gesture taking on an entirely new meaning. His rough cheeks against her soft skin, his warm lips so achingly close. She was reading far too much into it, of course. He kissed everyone like that—she'd seen it for herself.

It hit her then. Her earlier clumsiness and forgetfulness had nothing to do with the afternoon wine—it was something rather more basic and natural than that.

'Thank you, Fleur, for a wonderful day.' One hand was

still on her shoulder as his other hand tenderly made its way to her chin and gently tilted it so her eyes met his. As his face moved towards her she was as terrified and frozen as she'd been on that first day in Resus, except this time there was no question of her running. His lips moved towards her and found hers easily, kissing her full on her softly parted lips, and though it was short and sweet it could definitely not be interpreted as merely a friendly kiss, however loosely one defined the boundaries. 'Goodnight, Fleur,' he murmured softly.

Unable to speak—even 'goodnight' would have been like a tongue-twister—all Fleur could manage was a rather weak wave as Mario made his way to his car and drove off into the still, dark night.

It wasn't until she'd poured herself a rather large brandy and made her way out onto the decking that Fleur let herself breathe again. Well, that was probably stretching the medical possibility, she reasoned as she took a warming sip, but it certainly felt that way. The moon reflecting on the bay and the gently lapping sound of the waves didn't work their usual calming magic this time. Putting her hand to her cheeks, still burning from where he'd kissed her, Fleur's fingers moved to her lips. Closing her eyes for a moment, she relived the feeling of his mouth on hers, the scent of him close to her, his hands on her shoulders.

Of all the possibilities that going back to work had conjured up, of all the problems and emotions she'd known she might face, falling in love hadn't been one she'd considered.

'You don't love him,' Fleur said emphatically, out loud. 'You hardly know him. You're simply attracted to him.'

She stared out at the inky ocean as if defying it to contradict her, but the waves just carried on rolling in, the stars carried on twinkling and the world simply carried right on moving along, seemingly impervious to her plight.

CHAPTER FIVE

As MARIO had predicted, their 'date' had raised not a single eyebrow. Well, except for Kathy, but, then, she could have found someone to gossip with in the mortuary, Fleur reasoned. The department was obviously used to Mario's social antics, which was another reason for Fleur to keep her feelings firmly in check. It had been a simple kiss and no more. She was reading far too much into it.

Work improved steadily. Whether it was Mario that had instigated the change she couldn't be sure, but no longer were the patronising pats on the shoulder and 'there, theres' so evident. In fact, first thing on Monday morning she was summoned to Danny's office.

'We've been thinking...' he started.

'We?' Fleur questioned.

'Well, the bosses and I,' Danny replied, referring to the consultants and senior registrars. 'It's pointless trying to protect you in Obs and Section B. You know as well as I do that patients in A and E can deteriorate anywhere— even the most trivial wound can be masking something far more sinister. Hilda Green was a prime example. She's doing well, by the way. I rang Neuro and apparently she's being transferred to a rehabilitation hospital today. She's just got some residual right-sided weakness which they're hoping will resolve with aggressive physiotherapy.' He watched as Fleur smiled.

'I thought that might cheer you up.'

She didn't want to steal Danny's thunder by telling him that she knew already. When she'd dropped off Alex's urine sample yesterday Fleur had made a detour to the neuro ward to check for herself on Hilda's progress. Though the woman's speech had been slightly slurred, Fleur had been delighted to find her sitting out of bed, knitting. Not, of course, in the rapid fashion of the week before, but there was definitely a pink beanie in the making. If anyone was going to work hard at their recovery, Hilda was the woman for the job. Slowly but surely she would get there.

'Anyway,' Danny continued, 'what we thought, with your approval naturally, was that we'd throw you in at the deep end.' He looked at Fleur's stunned expression. 'With a lot of support, of course.'

'Are you trying to tell me that you want me to work in Resus?' Her lips were white as she comprehended the enormity of what Danny was suggesting.

'Look, Fleur, you're an A and E nurse through and through. No matter where you are in the department, given the nature of the job, if you want to be a patient's primary care-giver and follow them through, at some point Resus is where you're going to end up. Now, I'll be the first to admit I thought it would be too much for you, that the softly-softly approach was the way to go, but Mario was...' Fleur waited as Danny found the right words '...most insistent that my initial approach was the wrong one. He thought, I mean *we* thought that if you spent a couple of weeks exclusively in Resus it might be the best way of getting you back into the swing of things.'

So Mario *had* been the instigator. A surge of anger welled in Fleur. How insensitive was Mario? Even after she'd poured her heart out to him he obviously couldn't understand what she'd been through.

But deep down, and though it scared her to admit it at first, Fleur knew that this time the advice being offered was the right advice. In her two weeks back at work, it hadn't only been Hilda who'd taken a sudden turn for the worse. Little Amy Feathers, a tiny three-year-old with a sore throat, had suddenly started convulsing. A young girl with an asthma attack had rapidly worsened on her. And despite Fleur's relief at leaving them at the Resus door, it had also been tempered with frustration, a longing to follow her patients through, to be with them. It wasn't a feeling that could easily be defined, just the instincts of an emergency nurse—or a would-be emergency nurse once she overcame this final obstacle.

'When?' she said finally after the longest time. 'When do you want me to start in there?'

Danny gave her a relieved smile as he picked up his pager from the desk, but before he could answer a sharp rapping at the door interrupted them. Without waiting for Danny's response, Mario popped his head around the door. 'Danny, there's a chest pain coming in and there's no nurse down for Resus.'

Danny turned from Mario to Fleur. 'What do you say, Fleur? There's no time like the present.'

Looking at Mario's confused expression, Fleur tossed him an angry look. He may have been right to step in and effectively force her to face her demons, but there was no way he was getting off too lightly. 'I'll explain that particular proverb to you later, Mario. Thanks a bunch.'

Fleur managed a reassuring smile at her patient as the paramedics wheeled him in. 'Russel Parker, forty-five years of age, with sudden onset of central chest pain, radiating down his left arm. Past history of hypertension, hyperlipidaemia and a heavy smoker.' All this was said as they expertly aligned the ambulance stretcher with the resus bed. With Fleur and Danny's help, the paramedics lifted the rather obese man over as they reeled off the treatment they had instigated at the scene.

After thanking the paramedics, Fleur addressed her patient. 'Mr Parker, my name is Fleur Hadley. I'm the nurse who's going to be looking after you this morning, along with my colleague, Danny Miller. I'm just going to get you into a gown and attach you to our monitor while Mr Ruffini here, our emergency consultant, asks you some questions.'

The cardiac monitor Mr Parker was attached to was state of the art and new to Fleur. Under Danny's guidance Fleur was able to record the patient's blood pressure, oxygen saturation and print off a twelve-lead ECG, all at the touch of a few buttons.

'If you ask it nicely, it even makes a cup of tea,' Danny joked.

Mr Parker's ECG showed ST elevation which confirmed there was some acute cardiac event under way, but rather more ominous were several runs of rapid irregular heartbeats. Fleur noticed Mario's concerned glance at the monitor. 'Sister, would you mind paging Dr Lupen, the cardiology registrar? I might ask him to come down straight away. And could I have 5 mg of morphine.'

'Certainly.' She turned to Danny. 'You get the morphine while I page Dr Lupen.' Morphine was a controlled drug and required two staff members to check it, but Fleur knew without question that Mario would be happy to check the drugs with Danny if it meant his patient would be seen promptly by the specialist. Dr Lupen answered quickly and as Mario was examining Mr Parker's chest, Fleur briefly ran through the patient's history as she waited for Mario to come over.

'It's OK. Don't tear Mario away—just let him know I'm on my way down.' Dr Lupen, though friendly, usually only came down to Emergency on the direct request of a fellow doctor. However, the fact Mario was concerned was seemingly enough to merit Dr Lupen's appearance. Surprised at the ease of the referral, she replaced the receiver—more proof when none was needed that Mario commanded respect from everyone.

'Did you get him on the phone for me?' Mario asked as he pulled his stethoscope out of his ears.

'I explained the situation and he said he'd be down directly.'

He gave a murmur of thanks and returned his attention to the patient who was already starting to relax now the intravenous morphine was taking effect. 'So you are an ex-smoker, Mr Parker?' Fleur was just about to interrupt but held her tongue as Mr Parker shook his head.

'No, Doctor, I still smoke—unfortunately.'

But it soon became apparent that Mario hadn't misheard or misread the notes. 'No, Mr Parker. As of today you are an ex-smoker.'

'You're not wrong there, Doctor. I've had a heart attack, haven't I? I will be all right, though, won't I?' The fear was evident in his voice and again Mario didn't misread the signs. Fleur watched as Mario took his patient's hands, surprised by the gesture and even more taken back when Mr Parker, a tough Aussie in every sense of the word gripped it tightly.

'You *are* having a heart attack, Mr Parker, and I won't play games and tell you that there's nothing to worry about—that won't do either of us any good. But I can assure you that we have an excellent cardiac unit in this hospital, and Dr Lupen, the cardiology registrar who will see you shortly, is second to none. We will do our best to get you well and give you another chance. Then, my friend, it is up to you what you do with this chance. You understand what I am saying, yes?'

Mr Parker nodded, relaxing back on the pillows behind him, and Fleur again found herself in awe of Mario. His ability to simultaneously soothe the patient while delivering bad news was amazing, and not only that—he'd sown the seeds for educating Mr Parker, an essential part of cardiac rehabilitation.

The morning flew by. Busy? Yes. Exciting? Sometimes, but without any real major incident to test Fleur's nerves. Pleased with herself for coping, she knew deep down her moment of truth hadn't yet come. She felt as if she were riding on the dodgems, bumping around but getting there, with no real dangers apparent. Fleur also knew that her time could come at any moment, that the dodgem ride could quickly turn into a Formula 1 Grand Prix. As long as she was down for Resus, the lights could go on at any given moment and the real test of her skills would start. But when the chequered flag was waved, Fleur wondered, would she still be standing?

After changing into jeans and a T-shirt, she made her way through the department.

'One moment, Fleur.' Mario put down the telephone he was on and ran a couple of steps to catch up to her. 'I am finished here also, and I need to speak with you. Perhaps I could walk you to the car?'

'Sure.' Painfully aware of her rather faded jeans compared to his snappy suit, she slowed down and they walked along. 'How come you're finishing up now?'

Mario rolled his eyes. 'This afternoon I am child-sitting. It is Teresa and Marco's wedding anniversary and they are off to some luxury hotel. I can't moan really, it was my gift to them.' He took his notebook out of his pocket. 'I have to pick up Ricky at three-fifteen, swimming at four-thirty, homework, dinner and then do his reader with him, all before bed at eight! I think work would be a lot easier somehow.'

'And you needed to talk with me?'

'That was the path lab on the telephone, about Alex's urine sample.'

Fleur stopped in her tracks and swung round to face him. 'He's got an infection, or... He's not diabetic, is he?' A multitude of scenarios raced through her mind.

'No, Fleur, he's not diabetic, but he does appear to have a low-grade infection of his urine.'

Fleur let out a small wail of horror. 'But he must have had it for a couple of weeks. He might have some renal damage. I should—'

Mario's hands rested on her shoulders. He didn't shake her exactly but the weight of his touch stopped her gibbering. 'Stop,' he said firmly. 'First you need to collect a fresh specimen so they can confirm the findings, and as soon as you have done that we will hit him with a big dose of antibiotics. Next, I will make an appointment for him to see a urologist. Now, there probably is no damage, but you know yourself that urinary-tract infections in boys have to be investigated thoroughly. While you're waiting for the urologist appointment he'll have an ultrasound and an IVP to check his renal tract. All of which is common procedure. You must try not to worry until there's something to worry about.'

'But all this should all have been done a couple of weeks ago. I just assumed he was upset again and all this time he's had an infection. I should have known—'

'Fleur, you have to calm down.' Mario said firmly. 'He has a low-grade infection. Stop imagining the worse, and stop blaming yourself. It was perfectly natural to assume that his bed-wetting was because he was upset, given that you were starting work again and the problems Alex is having with friends. You have to stop trying to be his GP, counsellor, teacher and footy coach and just let yourself be his mum.'

She looked up at him, bemused. 'What do you mean?'

'Just that. You're running yourself ragged, trying to take the blame for everything and compensate for all that has happened. You need to see what a fantastic job you are doing and stop imagining the worse.'

Fleur stiffened at the rather backhanded compliment. 'I think you're being rather premature in drawing your conclusions about me, Mario. We've barely known each other for more than a couple of weeks.' His hands were still on her shoulders and Fleur was suddenly conscious of his touch, casting her eyes down she waited for the next tirade of 'calm down' and 'don't blame yourself'. It was easy for a man to dictate—they weren't the ones saddled with the bottomless goody-bag of hormones and guilt the beaming midwife handed to you along with the baby.

'Has it really only been two weeks?' The genuine bewilderment in his voice made her look up. 'I feel I have known you so much longer.'

Her mind drifted back to Saturday night, standing on the balcony, and the emotions that had coursed through her then. Could so much have happened for both of them in such a short space of time? An unflattering blush was starting to spread.

His hands had been there far too long. Shrugging them off, Fleur swallowed hard a couple of times. His voice, his eyes, his touch—they were all doing the strangest things to her. She needed some distance, she needed to get in to her car and back to the relative safety of worrying about Alex—not be standing in the car park, blushing like some gauche teenager. 'Yes, just two weeks,' Fleur said rather too sharply. 'Which in my opinion is rather too early for someone to be questioning my parenting skills.' She had gone too far—again—but there was no way she was going to back down.

'Here.' He handed her a bag which she took without comment. 'There's a specimen container and a pathology slip and some antibiotics. Is Alex allergic to penicillin?'

Fleur shook her head.

'Good. I'll arrange the investigations.' And with a rather curt nod he turned on his extremely well-shod heel and left her.

Damn, damn, damn. Terrified of betraying too much, she'd behaved like an ungrateful brat. Muttering furiously to herself, Fleur managed to stall the car. Of course, Mario's sleek silver BMW had to be behind her. Grinding the gears and putting her foot down way too hard, she jerked out of the car park in a puff of smoke, absolutely refusing to look in the rear-view mirror at what would undoubtedly be his gorgeous, totally unruffled, smooth expression.

It didn't take long to calm down, a cup of Earl Grey and a few chocolate biscuits, in fact. Fleur knew she had to apologise to Mario for her behaviour. But at the school gates a mother trying to rope Fleur in to help with the uniform shop accosted her.

Pleading that she'd just started work as her reason for not being able to help, Fleur cast her eyes across the playground to where Mario stood by the flagpole.

'It really would only be for a couple of hours a week,' the mother insisted.

'Look, I'd honestly love to but now is just not a good time.' The bell sounded and Fleur gratefully left before she had to plead temporary insanity and a tendency to kleptomania to get out of the most hated job on the school's PTA list.

Crossing a playground was quite a hazardous task when two hundred and fifty over-excited school children were running at great speed across your path. By the time she'd made it to the flagpole, Mario and Ricky were calmly walking hand in hand to the car park. Oh, well, it would keep until tomorrow.

The boys were in great spirits, and for once Fleur relented and let them play cricket outside instead of tackling their homework. Only when Ben had been fetched by Kathy and they had the place to themselves did Fleur tell Alex the news and collect the sample before she gave him his first tablet.

Surprisingly, Alex seemed delighted at the news he had an infection. 'So it's not my fault that I'm wetting the bed?'

Fleur shook her head, glad at least that one of them was pleased.

'And the antibiotics will fix it?'

'Yes. But as I explained, you'll have to have a few tests and see a specialist. Infections like this are a bit more uncommon in boys than girls, so the doctor will just want to check that everything is in good working order and make sure there's no underlying problem that's causing you to get an infection.'

'The same tests I had when I first started wetting?'

'Mostly.'

Alex grinned. 'Well, I had two kidneys then. I remember the doctor showing me and he said everything else was normal. I bet it's all fine.'

It was like a bucket of water being poured over her. Why had it taken a seven-year-old to state the obvious, when his own mother a qualified nurse at that hadn't even thought it? Sure, the tests might show up something, but her nightmarish visions of missing kidneys and malformed ureters were completely unfounded. She was completely and utterly overreacting. Sure, a urinary tract infection wasn't good news exactly but she *was* being a touch dramatic. Mario had definitely been right.

Her chance to apologise didn't have to wait. Just as she was surveying the fridge and wondering what to cook, the phone rang. Mario's accent was instantly recognisable, but his agitated ramblings weren't.

'I am sorry to disturb you, I am just so confused.'

'Mario, I'm actually glad that you did. I was hoping to see you at the school. I really am sorry about earlier. I know you were trying to be nice and help.'

'Don't worry about that. I really need your help.'

'My help?' Fleur pulled the receiver from her ear and stared at it for a second. 'Why?'

'Have you seen the children's homework tonight?'

She had to strain to catch what he was saying.

'Mario, why are you whispering?'

'Because Ricky is in the other room, waiting for me to come and help him. I am a doctor, yes? Supposedly clever, yes? Yet I can't help a seven-year-old with his homework.'

Reaching over the bench, Fleur unzipped Alex's schoolbag, retrieving his homework book and flicked through it.

'What is this "Stitch in time saves nine"? And "A rolling stone gathers no moss"?'

Fleur started to laugh as she understood his utter confusion. 'They have to explain the meaning of these proverbs, like the one I told you about at Auskick.'

'That much I understand, but listen to this one. "A bird in the hand is worth two in the bush." What the hell are they going on about?'

Trying and failing not to gurgle with laughter at his

bemusement, Fleur forced herself to stop when she heard his hurt voice on the other end of the line.

'You're laughing at me! If that's the reaction from a full-grown woman, can you just imagine what Ricky is going to do? This whole evening has been a disaster. I promised him some good Italian carbonara and I forget to get eggs, and now this!'

'I'm sorry.' Fleur pulled a poker face, as she wiped away a tear. 'Look, bring Ricky over here and the boys can do their homework together. I'll make dinner, though heaven knows what. My routine has vanished since I went back to work. Maybe we can ring for a pizza?'

'You have eggs?'

Even that sounded funny at the moment but Fleur managed not to slip back into her earlier hysterics. 'Yes, I have eggs,' she replied, but the humour was wasted on him.

'Then I shall bring the rest of the ingredients and while you help the boys I will make dinner.'

'Sounds great.'

Which gave her about eight minutes to do the quickest tidy in history, brush her hair and teeth and apply a quick slick of lipstick. Alex pulled her up just as she was spilling a bottle of perfume over her wrists.

'What are you doing, Mum?' Alex asked accusingly.

'Nothing.' She flushed guiltily. 'Just making the place presentable. Mario's bringing Ricky over to do his homework with you.'

'So why are you putting on perfume?'

Why indeed? Thankfully she was saved from answering by the doorbell.

'Where's the car?' Alex asked as they traipsed in, laden with bags.

'We walked,' Ricky said moodily.

'Of course we walked. Fleur and Alex are just ten

minutes away. We're practically neighbours.' Handing her a brown paper bag with a bottle inside, they all made their way into the kitchen.

The next half-hour was spent with Fleur yet again explaining proverbs as Mario noisily busied himself banging saucepans, chopping onions and mushrooms with lightning speed and generally creating a pretty stunning backdrop.

'"Home is where the heart is"?' Ricky said chewing on his pencil.

'Well...imagine you're on camp,' Fleur said, thinking on her feet.

'Huh! I wouldn't be allowed to go.' Alex chimed in.

'Imagine you were, and you were allowed to ring home. You might be missing me. And if you were a bit quiet later that evening, it might be because you were thinking about home and your nice things and the people you love. And even though you were having a great time at camp and enjoying being with your friends, you'd realise that what makes a home is the people you love. That's where your heart is.'

Alex gave her a horrified look as Ricky laughed, egging him on. 'No way! I'd be enjoying camp too much.'

'OK, bad example. Um, I know, take Mario! He might be living in Australia at the moment and having a wonderful time, but say he had a lady friend in Rome that he was in love with and missed a lot.'

The boys started whistling and cheering as Mario dramatically put his hand to his heart and pretended to wipe away a tear.

'Well, his heart would be in Rome with his lady friend. Rome would be his home because that's where his heart belongs.'

'So what do we write?' Ricky asked, his pencil poised.

'Work it out for yourself.' Fleur grinned. 'You know

what it means now.' Crossing the room, she watched as Mario stirred the creamy sauce. 'That smells marvellous. The boys are just finishing up. I'll lay the table.'

Pulling a corkscrew out of the drawer, she opened the paper bag. 'Cranberry juice!'

Mario gave her an apologetic grin. 'It's supposed to be great for the urinary tract—he should drink some every day.'

'Oh.'

Rummaging in a carrier bag, he pulled out another bottle and with a wink he handed it to her. 'It's a little bit darker in colour than the cranberry juice but a lot more inviting. I think you deserve it after tackling all those proverbs.'

'I'll say.'

Dinner was delicious, the wine was gorgeous, the kids' manners were atrocious and it was the best meal Fleur had enjoyed for ages. They talked and laughed and told stupid jokes—and that was just the adults. So engrossed in each other were they that Fleur hardly noticed when the boys scampered off to the study to use the computer. Naturally they had a coffee, and then another, and by then the news had started so they drifted through to the lounge and caught up on world affairs, finding out each other's political persuasions and the like.

It was only when Ricky and Alex appeared yawning and obviously worn out that they realised the time.

'Teresa will never forgive me, keeping him up till ten on a school night.'

Bundling him out of the door, Mario turned. 'Thank you, Fleur, for your help.'

'No, Mario, thank you, and sorry about earlier.'

He flicked his hand dismissively, his gold bracelet catching the light. 'I enjoy a little row now and then, and with a feisty lady like you I guess I'd better get used to it.'

He kissed her on both cheeks, a ritual she was coming to appreciate more and more by the day. She closed her eyes as his lips brushed her cheek, filled with a desire to once again feel his lips on hers, her breathing quickening at the physical contact.

'Come on, Uncle Mario.'

There was no repeat of the other night—their audience put paid to that—but Fleur knew, just *knew* that he wanted her lips on his, too. 'What are you on tomorrow?' Mario asked gruffly.

'A late shift. You?'

His eyes bored into hers. 'I'm sure I can find a reason to hang around.'

Fleur's eyes boldly held his gaze as he awaited her response. 'Let's hope so,' she replied huskily.

After getting an exhausted Alex into his pyjamas, and giving him another tablet, for the first time in living memory she didn't rush off to the kitchen and tidy up, or set about getting everything ready for the morning—it could all wait. Instead, she ran herself the longest, deepest bath and lit a few candles, gazing dreamily at the ceiling as the liquid gold voice of Bocelli filled the steamy air, trying to fathom out why life suddenly felt wonderful...

CHAPTER SIX

THE chequered flag wasn't waved during Fleur's two-week spell in Resus. The gods that dictated these matters seemed to have colluded to ensure that all the major dramas came in when Fleur was either safely at home or at the very least had made it out to the car park. Sure, there were a few hairy moments, but nothing that really tested her, and gradually with her colleagues' help Fleur's inner confidence strengthened.

So when a multiple injury from a motor vehicle accident was wheeled in early one afternoon, five weeks after Fleur had started back at the hospital, she was able to detach herself enough to deal with the trauma in a calm, professional manner. Even though the patient's injuries were similar to Rory's, Fleur was so busy holding the unfortunate woman's neck in position as she was lifted over onto the bed that she simply didn't have time to dwell on the fact. In fact, she was so busy pulling up drugs for the anaesthetist, as well as setting up for an emergency chest tube, that by the time the reality of what she'd just witnessed hit home, the patient was being speedily wheeled up to Theatre with Danny and the team of surgeons, leaving Fleur alone in Resus with a grinning Mario.

'You were marvellous,' Mario enthused as he pulled off his blood-soaked gloves and aimed them at the metal bucket.

Fleur gave him a cheeky grin. 'I was, wasn't I? Danny's got a meeting with Admin when he gets back and he's going to leave me with the pager.' To the uninitiated it didn't sound like a great deal. But while she held the little black bleeper, it would be Fleur who would co-ordinate the initial response to whatever came through the unit's door.

Mario at once realised the significance of Fleur agreeing to this: she was back in the swing of things, ready to take on the responsibilities of before.

'Now, that really is marvellous.' He smiled. 'So marvellous, in fact, that I would go as far as to say the lady deserves a glass of champagne to celebrate.'

'Oh, you would, huh? And what if the lady in question didn't happen to have any champagne?'

Mario furrowed his forehead, as if deep in thought. 'Then I suppose I'd have to go and get some, already chilled, of course, and perhaps bring it around to her home.'

Until now, Mario had never once pushed her but Fleur could feel the tension building between them—an ever-increasing aura around them, a need to be alone, to explore each other, to see if this really was going anywhere.

Sure, he had been at her house a couple of times, shared a barbie or three with her and Alex, but it was now time to move things forward. She *wanted* things to move forward.

So when Mario offered to bring champagne over, it was a slightly nervous Fleur that hid behind her fringe as she restocked the IV cupboard. 'Perhaps around nine—that way the lady could be sure her son was in bed.'

Peeking out from behind her blonde curtain, she saw the huge smile on his face. 'You're sure?' he checked tentatively, unable to keep the note of excitement out of his deep voice.

'I'm sure.'

'I'm bringing a child down from Section B.' Felicity's

voice, crackling over the intercom, made them both jump. It had that note of urgency that needed no further explanation. Fleur's reflexes were like lightning. Felicity rushed past and laid a naked boy down on the resus bed as Fleur checked his vital signs. Looking over the bruised, bleeding body, she saw that the child was breathing, but only just. His pulse was difficult to palpate and extremely rapid and thready. Mario was already tying a tourniquet around the limp, pale arm and trying unsuccessfully to establish IV access.

Suctioning the patient's mouth to remove some secretions, she inserted an airway and placed a paediatric oxygen mask over his nose and mouth.

'What the story?' Mario asked, as again he attempted to insert an IV bung.

Fleur was fairly sure she knew the answer to his question already, but the errant nature of Accident and Emergency was yet again rammed home when Felicity answered, 'The family dog bit him.' Felicity's voice was shaking. 'His mum was lined up at Reception with him wrapped in a towel—she thought that was what you had to do, and, not realising, Reception sent them to me.'

Which would have been awful for Felicity, Fleur knew. Section B was for the walking wounded. To pull back a towel and see a child in this state would have been a terrible shock.

Mario swore softly as his third attempt at gaining IV access failed. The boy's veins were hopelessly collapsed.

'He needs fluids now! I'm going to have to set up for an intraosseous infusion.'

Fleur nodded, reaching for the rarely used intraosseous pack. 'Have you seen this used before, Felicity?' Felicity shook her head as various staff gathered around the bed, attaching the child to monitors, running through IVs.

'Someone, take the mother to the interview room, get as much information as you can from her—a name for the child, too.' Felicity made to go but Fleur called her back.

'Felicity, I want you to stay and watch this. Lucy can talk to the mother.

'Now, as you can see, Mario is unable to get IV access. Because the child is so shocked, his veins are very hard to find. Rather than waste time, he's going to commence what's called an intraosseous infusion.' The conversation was taking place as Fleur assisted Mario, passing him an alcohol swab and then the needle. 'By inserting the needle directly into a bone, in this case the anterior aspect of the tibia, bloods can be taken for cross-matching and drugs given through this route, as well as IV fluids. We can run an infusion directly into the marrow cavity. It's very effective and very quick, as you can see.'

Bloods were taken for cross-matching and a plasma substitute was gently pushed through the needle in the child's leg as the monitors relayed their messages. Mario swiftly assessed the injuries as Fleur relayed his observations. 'His oxygen saturation was seventy-four per cent on arrival but is now ninety per cent on ten litres of oxygen. He's tachycardic at one hundred and forty, and his blood pressure is sixty on thirty. Do you want us to emergency page the paediatricians?'

Mario nodded. 'His abdomen's rigid. Get the surgeons down here, too.'

'Right. Felicity, dial triple 0 and ask the operator to fast-page the on-call surgical and paediatric teams to come to Accident and Emergency.'

Lucy, who had taken the mother off to the interview room, returned with an update. 'His name is Archie Levitski, and the dog he was bitten by was a pit bull terrier. Apparently Archie must have wandered out into the garden. He was supposed to be having his afternoon sleep and his mother had just hung out some washing. She thought she'd locked the patio door but she must have made a mistake.'

Mario muttered something rather loud in Italian. Though Fleur spoke not a single word of the language, his utterance left no one in the room in any doubt as to what he'd just said. 'Let's get some sterile saline dressings over his wounds. They're not bleeding much—I expect that's because he's so shut down. Undoubtedly he's bleeding internally. Where the hell are the paeds?'

Danny came back from Theatre at that moment, but Fleur was too busy to acknowledge his return. Holding the boy's chin up to maintain his airway, Fleur felt Archie stiffen beneath her. His eyes suddenly opened and then rolled back into his head as he started to convulse.

'Mario, he's starting to fit,' she said, rolling Archie onto his side.

'He's vomiting.' Mario stated, but Fleur had already seen that coming and she reached for the suction catheter, working quickly in a desperate attempt to prevent Archie from aspirating.

'Valium now,' Mario barked. 'Lucy, go back to the mother and find out if he's ever had a fit before, and find out about any drug allergies. Someone, put out a paediatric crash call.'

'He hasn't arrested,' Danny stated calmly. 'An emergency page would be more appropriate.'

'*Maledetto!*' The same expletive that had graced their ears previously again filled the room, only this time it was aimed directly at Danny.

'I don't believe we have that drug in the trolley, Mario,' Danny said calmly.

'You expect me to wait until he arrests?' Mario shouted.

Fleur never once looked up from Archie. Technically she couldn't pull rank over Danny—he was in charge after all—but this afternoon she was down for Resus and this little guy was *her* patient and Fleur was going to do the right thing by him.

'Danny, put out a paediatric arrest, please.' Her voice was clear, unwavering, and she carried on dealing with Archie as she spoke.

Almost imperceptibly and only for an instant the room stilled, and then she heard Danny pick up the phone.

Lucy ran in, breathless. 'He's epileptic.'

'Good.' It sounded a strange thing for Mario to say, but the fact that there was a medical reason for the convulsion lessened the likelihood that the fit had been caused because of neurological damage from the dog attack.

'Thanks, Lucy.' Fleur nodded her appreciation. 'Stay and watch now, and I'll go over everything with you later.'

'Paediatric arrest in Accident and Emergency. Paediatric arrest in Accident and Emergency.' Danny's pager duly sprang into life and was joined in loud stereo as paediatric teams swung through the doors, alerted by the earlier page.

'Not an arrest, guys,' Mario said quickly, 'but we need you.'

As the second on-call anaesthetist and surgeons arrived—the first on were still in Theatre—the room quickly filled, all working in an urgent attempt to stabilise this tiny life that hung in the balance.

'Fleur…' Danny came over to the head of the bed. 'I should push off to this meeting. Are you sure you don't mind?'

So absorbed was Fleur in what she was doing that she barely had time to nod. He slipped the pager into her pocket and Fleur felt the weight of it in her linen top. She didn't have time to be nervous, didn't have time to fear the weight of responsibility that had descended on her shoulders—she was simply doing her job. And as Archie's blood pressure started to creep up and his heart rate settled to a less alarming rate, as his reflexes picked up and his breathing steadied, Fleur acknowledged internally that she was doing her job well.

Blood was given and antibiotics were commenced as the bites would be a huge source of infection. As the oxygen, drugs and fluids started to infiltrate Archie's system, his condition steadied and the discussion as to his further treatment commenced. 'I'm going to ring Luke.'

Fleur looked up at Mario's words. 'He's off this afternoon.'

Mario nodded. 'He's the man at the top. I know that I'd want to be informed about a child as sick as this little guy. Once the press gets hold of this it's going to be plastered everywhere.'

He was absolutely right, Fleur thought. Luke Richardson did indeed deserve a courtesy call, yet many, too many, would have let ego come into it. Would have wanted to be the one who ran the show, who dealt with the press. Mario was a true team player—most of the time.

'Then I will talk with the mother. It sounds as if they want to transfer him to the Women's and Children's.' He looked over at Phil Sawyer, the paediatric consultant, who nodded.

'He's obviously going to need intensive care, and our beds are full—or at least they will be when the MVA gets out of Theatre. Is that right, Wendy?'

Wendy looked up briefly from Archie whose abdomen she was examining. 'It sounds that way. If we can arrange the helicopter, we can have him there in less than half an hour. I think he'd do better being transferred now rather than post-op. He's stabilising and a paediatric intensive care ward would be better. And also Mr Hassed is there,' she added. Mr Hassed was one of the most eminent plastic surgeons in Australia. Now that Archie's circulation was improving, the lacerations were starting to fill with blood and bruising was coming out all over his tiny body. The true horror of the child's injuries were becoming apparent. Wendy's voice was suddenly thick with emotion. 'This little guy is going to need all the help he can get.'

Mario looked down at the little boy, and suddenly the hot-headed, demanding doctor seemed to drain out of him. He stood there for a second, a pensive look flicking across his face, his features suddenly weary. But almost immediately his melancholy was over and normal services were resumed. 'Do you want me to arrange it?' he asked briskly, and without waiting for an answer marched out of the room.

By the time Mario had arranged for the air ambulance and spoken with Luke, Danny had returned.

'They cancelled the meeting. Apparently, the meeting room hadn't been serviced and, more to the point, the canteen had forgotten to send up the refreshments. Those admin guys want to spend a couple of days in this place— no one's even had a coffee-break yet.'

Mario rolled his eyes as he walked over. 'Please, don't mention coffee again until I have a cup in my hand. Fleur, will you come with me while I speak with the mother?'

Fleur looked up briefly at Danny. 'Can you keep an eye on Archie? He's stable, but Felicity is pretty upset and Lucy, as good as she is, is still just a student.'

Danny nodded. 'Sure, I'd rather be in here than with the mother. Are you sure you'll be all right, Fleur?'

'She'll be fine,' Mario answered for her rather testily. 'Come on, Fleur.'

Danny pursed his lips but didn't rise. 'Good luck.'

As they reached the interview room Mario paused for a moment. The muscles in his cheeks were taut, his lips set in a grim line. He took a couple of deep breaths and Fleur watched as his features relaxed. Catching her watching him inquisitively, Mario gave her a small smile.

'Excuse me, but I'm not looking forward to this.' His hand reached out and touched her bare arm. 'If I come on too strong, please, Fleur, interrupt me. I don't want to make things worse for the woman, but—'

'I understand Mario.' And she did, only too well. Theirs was not to judge or reason, but sometimes it was a tough call.

Mrs Levitski barely acknowledged their entrance. She sat rocking gently in the chair, wringing the blood-splattered towel over and over in her hands. Fleur noticed the chewed nails and the untouched cup of tea.

'Mrs Levitski, my name is Mario Ruffini. I am the emergency consultant and this is Sister Fleur Hadley. We have been looking after your son.'

Mrs Levitski didn't look up or speak. Moving the cup, Mario sat down on the coffee-table in front of her. 'Mrs Levitski,' he said softly.

Her eyes lifted and met his. Terrified eyes, brimming with unshed tears. It was as if she had only just realised there were people in the room. 'Don't tell me he's dead. Please, don't—'

Immediately Mario reassured her. 'No, he's not dead.' He paused for a moment, allowing the one piece of good news in the whole sorry saga to sink in before he continued. 'He is a sick little boy, though, Mrs Levitski. I need for you to tell me exactly what happened.'

She nodded, swallowing hard to compose herself before she spoke, her voice a hoarse whisper. 'He's such a good dog, never bitten anyone, not even snapped or growled, well, not at us anyway. There's been a lot of break-ins around our way.'

Fleur glanced down at the admission sheet she was holding and looked at the address. Delvue Waters was notorious for vandalism and crime so she could understand Mrs Levitski's fear, yet she had to stop herself from visibly wincing as Mrs Levitski continued. 'The children climb all over him, treat him like a little pony.'

'What happened today?' Mario asked.

'I put Archie down for his sleep and then I went to hang out the washing. I did a bit of tidying up and then I went to do the dishes. That's when I saw him lying there on the grass.'

The room fell silent and Fleur watched as Mario stared down at his hands for a moment. 'Did you hear Archie scream?' Fleur prompted gently.

'No, nothing, not a sound. He was just lying there. I was looking out the window, half daydreaming and that's when I saw him. The dog wasn't even near him. For a second, as I was running out to him, I thought he must have tripped and fallen, but he was so still...' She started to cry in earnest. 'I was calling his name and he just lay there, not moving. As soon as I turned him over I knew what had happened.' She started to rock again, retreating into her own private hell.

'And where was the dog at this time?' Mario's voice was sharp without being unkind, dragging her back to the story.

'In his kennel, playing with his bone like nothing had happened. I picked Archie up and ran inside. I didn't know what to do. The phone's been cut off so I couldn't call an ambulance. I just grabbed a towel and put him in the car and raced up here. I should have gone to a neighbour, I just didn't think. It's all my fault, all of it...'

And as Mario reached over and for the first time touched the woman, his beautiful olive hands gently reaching her shoulders, Fleur knew he felt it, too—not anger, not bitterness, just an overwhelming feeling of sadness. Mrs Levitski did love her son. She was probably doing her best and doing it tough. She had, like so many others, just assumed it could never happen to her, that their dog was somehow different.

'Maybe Archie disturbed the dog when he was chewing his bone, or tripped and somehow frightened the dog. I cannot say. But I must tell you this...' His accent was pronounced but his words were clear. 'Archie has serious injuries, some of them internal. That means he is bleeding inside and needs to go to Theatre. My colleagues and I feel he would do better at the Women and Children's Hospital, and now that he is more stable we are going to transfer him there for his operation. But first I need to ask some questions. I see that Archie is nearly four years of age. He had a prolonged seizure shortly after he came in to us. A fit,' he explained as Mrs Levitski frowned.

'He gets them sometimes.'

'Apart from the fits, is Archie a well child?'

'He's a bit behind, a bit slow, you know. The doctor says it's to do with the fits, but now they're better controlled he's catching up. He's nearly toilet trained and he knows all his colours and can count. We go to speech therapy twice a week. This isn't going to help, is it?'

'We'll have to wait and see,' Mario said softly. 'Now, the helicopter will be ready to take him soon. In cases such as this the police will need to speak with you. They will take you in a car to the other hospital so you get there quickly.' He glanced up at Fleur who was about to interrupt, worried he might be making a promise he couldn't deliver. 'I arranged this when I arranged the ambulance.'

'The dog will have to be destroyed,' Mrs Levitski said suddenly. It was a statement, not a question, and Fleur felt relief that Mrs Levitski was being sensible. 'Can I see Archie—before he goes, I mean?'

'Of course, I will take you to him now.' Taking Mrs Levitski's elbow, Mario helped her up and then he did the strangest thing, considering that he was a doctor, considering his anger only moments before. He wrapped his arms around Mrs Levitski's scruffy, heaving shoulders and held her for a moment while she wept. And as Fleur watched, a tear fell down her own cheek. That one small gesture, the comfort of human touch, had somehow formed a small shield around Mrs Levitski. He had accepted her for what she was—a grief-stricken mother. He had listened without judging and had shown compassion when it had been needed. And in the awful days that would inevitably follow—the police interviews, the scathing press reports, the emotive public debates—it would be something for Mrs Levitski to cling to.

'How are you feeling, Fleur?'

'I'm fine, Felicity. How about you?'

'Actually, I'm still shaking. Do you need a hand to clean up Resus?'

Fleur shook her head. 'No, you go and grab a coffee, and perhaps you could bring one back for Mario when you're done. He's starting to have withdrawal symptoms.' She gestured over to Mario who was writing up his notes in the corner.

'Double strength,' he called as Felicity left. 'These notes will take ages.'

'Well, be sure to write neatly,' Fleur said as tactfully as she could. 'You'll probably have to do a police report.'

'Good point,' Mario agreed. 'Even I can't read my handwriting sometimes.' He looked over and put down his pen. 'Are you sure you're OK, Fleur? You did a great job.'

Fleur nodded. 'I'm fine, so long as you haven't forgotten about the champagne.'

He didn't get a chance to answer as Danny strolled in. 'How are you doing, Fleur? Is there anything you want to go over?'

'Honestly, Danny, I'm fine.'

'In that case, why don't you go and have a break? I'll finish up here.'

It was good to have friends, Fleur thought as she attempted to make her way to the coffee-room. But when every staff member she passed, even Len the porter, enquired how she felt, Fleur thought her face would crack when she smiled and assured them all that, no, she wasn't about to fall on the floor in a heap and, yes, she was fine, thank you!

Felicity was making her way back with Mario's favourite brew and as Fleur sat down, slipped her shoes off and took a grateful sip of her steaming drink, she nodded to Wendy, who was obviously taking a well-earned break. But her casual hello died on her lips when she saw that Wendy was crying. Not loud, obvious tears, but her reddened eyes and nose and a couple of mascara smudges were a pretty fair indication.

'Wendy.' Instantly Fleur stood up and made her way over, taking a seat beside the other woman.

'I'm sorry.' Wendy shook her head and blew her nose loudly. 'That young nurse that was just in was pretty upset and I was going over it all with her and it just got to me all of a sudden. Luckily I managed to hold off the tears until she'd gone.'

'There's nothing wrong with having a cry. We're all upset.'

Wendy shrugged. 'It doesn't seem that way. Oh, I know that you are, I know everyone is really, but it just seems to me that once you put on this white coat you're not supposed to have feelings any more, or at least not show them.'

'Wendy, we have debriefings here. Everyone gets together and goes over—'

'How many doctors come?' Wendy's voice was suddenly angry. 'And if they do, they only stay for the medical side of things. Those debriefings are to comfort the junior staff who haven't seen this type of thing. And it's not just the doctors who hold back. I know for sure that Danny never gets upset at those meetings and I bet that if you do, you hold it back.'

She had a point there. No one senior really let down their guards at these meetings, and though Admin would never in a million years admit it, if they were to, it would be seen as a sign of weakness.

'But there's the weekly team meeting for the senior staff,' Fleur reasoned. 'And we all go out every few weeks to have a drink and unwind. It's not just in the debriefing sessions.'

'But what's the golden rule on those evenings? What's the first thing we say as we go up to the bar? "Let's not talk about work."'

'Tonight I'll go home,' Wendy continued bitterly, 'and my husband will ask what sort of day I've had. And, of course, I'll just moan it was busy or something, without telling him what hell it really was.'

'So why not tell him?'

Wendy gave a hollow laugh. 'He doesn't like the gory bits. Anyway, his answer would be, "Don't do it, then." He's hoping I'll give up soon to have a family. I love being a doctor, I love nearly everything about it, but I tell you this much—nothing in medical school prepares you for having your feelings dredged every single day and nothing in this hospital is really set in place to help. That little boy was one of the most tragic things I've ever seen and, apart from you, who will I talk about it with? I mean *really* talk about it. Who will Phil Sawyer and Mario Ruffini talk about it with? Sure, we'll get updates and make a few casual comments, and that, Fleur, will be that. Down to business, onto the next one.'

It hit Fleur then. Wendy was right, she was so very right, and she, Fleur, was as guilty as anyone. How many times had she said she was fine on her walk to the coffee-room? Instead of having a cry, a rave at the injustice of the world, she had forced a smile and carried on. And what was worse, far worse, was she'd done it safe in the knowledge that tonight Mario would be there for her, holding her, soothing her, when finally she did let her guard down.

But what about Mario? Who was going to be comforting him? Fleur cast her mind back, remembering the pensive look on his face, the agony of his conversation with Mrs Levitski.

Scribbling her phone number down, Fleur pressed it into Wendy's hand. 'Come round at the weekend for a coffee or whatever your poison is and we'll have a proper chat.'

'You won't say anything?'

Fleur sighed. 'That's the whole problem, Wendy, no one ever says anything. But don't worry—this conversation stays in this room.'

Wendy smiled. 'Thanks, Fleur, I'll give you a buzz.'

As Fleur entered Resus she saw Mario there still diligently writing, but now she could see the tension in his shoulders, the deep lines around his eyes as he struggled to put down on paper what he'd just witnessed. Walking over, she placed a tender hand on his shoulder.

'How are you doing there, Mario?'

'Nearly done. I've just got to write up the drugs we gave.'

Fleur squeezed the knotted muscles beneath her fingers. 'I mean, how are *you* doing? It was pretty upsetting in there.'

And though she was standing behind him, she could feel a smile on his lips as his hand reached out and grabbed hers, holding it there on his shoulder. 'It was bloody awful,' he sighed. 'Hell, I might even bring two bottles tonight.'

CHAPTER SEVEN

'LOOK, Mum.' Alex waved a card cheerfully as he ran over. 'Ricky's invited me to his party. Please, say I can go.'

Fleur read the invite as they walked over to the car. The party was next Friday and Alex had been invited to don his pyjamas for a night of fast food and videos and, to cap it off, a take-away breakfast the following morning from the nearby burger bar.

'There's going to be four other boys, including Ricky, so I'm really lucky to get invited. Ricky said that his mum would ring you with all the details later in the week. But I am going to be able to go, Mum, aren't I?'

There wasn't a logical reason on earth why he shouldn't. From the second day of antibiotics he hadn't had a wet bed and Teresa was a lovely responsible woman who had obviously pre-empted that Fleur would want to talk with her. Fleur started the car engine as Alex looked at her expectantly.

'OK, you can go...' She held up her hand as the squeals of delight started. 'But you and I will be having a big talk before then about how you behave in other people's houses, especially if you're staying the night.'

'Sure. Hey, Mum, you'll have the whole house to yourself. What will you do?'

Fleur laughed. 'Worry about you. What else?'

So determined was Alex not to jeopardise his chances of going to the party that Fleur had absolutely no problem getting him to bed early. In fact, by seven-thirty she was working herself into a state, wondering what on earth she'd been doing suggesting to Mario this evening alone together. What were they going to talk about without the relative safety of Alex and, worse still, what if talking was the last thing on Mario's mind? What then?

Walking over to the mantelpiece, she took down her wedding picture. There was Rory, so straight and proud, his blond hair shining in the afternoon sun, his green eyes smiling down at his new bride. Fleur examined her image carefully. How young and carefree she'd looked, her hair piled up loosely on her head, peppered with gypsophila, her blue eyes gazing adoringly back at Rory. Clear blue eyes, she noted. No early lines or dark circles like now. No real cares or worries then, just all the promise that tomorrow held.

'Oh, Rory,' she whispered. 'I miss you so much. Why did you have to leave us?' How long she stood there, staring at the photo, she couldn't be sure, but certainly long enough to realise that though the passage of time had soothed the initial pain, nothing could diminish her grief for all she had lost. And now here she was, inviting someone new into her life, moving on, not in leaps or bounds but with slow, painful steps that terrified her. There were so many uncertainties, so much to deal with. She wanted Mario, wanted him to kiss her. To deny it would be a lie, but what then? Would she be thinking of Rory, imagining it was him in her arms? Comparing them?

'Do you understand, Rory?' she whispered. 'Tell me I'm doing the right thing.' She stared harder, searching for what she wasn't sure—an answer, a sign? But, of course, pictures didn't answer, pictures didn't always paint a thousand words. With a sigh Fleur replaced the picture on the mantelpiece. A thousand words would be wonderful, she mused, but right now she'd settle for just one…

True to his word, Mario brought two bottles, and as they curled up on the sofa and tucked into a risotto Fleur had prepared, she thanked the heavens for her earlier conversation with Wendy. How easy it would have been otherwise to have spoken only about herself—how the day had affected her, how she'd coped with the grief of Rory on top of the MVA and Archie. But Wendy's words had hit a nerve so, instead of answering Mario's concerned questions and exploring her own emotions, she had the foresight to turn the tables and ask Mario about himself—how he felt, how he reacted to the endless demands on his spirit. She was rewarded a hundred times over as gradually, piece by piece, he filled her in on his life, his feelings and his family back in Rome.

'My mother is the typical Italian mother. Gorgeous, of course, feeds me way too much, worries endlessly about the fact that I'm not married and giving her hundreds of grandchildren to dote over and thoroughly spoil.'

Fleur laughed. 'And what about your father?'

'He is a doctor also, a physician. He works far too hard and ignores his own health, which hasn't been too good lately. He's a wonderful man.'

'Does he worry too—about you not being married, I mean?'

'He says no, but deep down I think he is just as bad as my mother is. I'm well into my thirties now, as my mother keeps reminding me. She keeps thrusting these single women at me and, of course, then I "shame" both families by not asking the lady out for a second date.'

'Why? I mean, are they awful—the girls your family sets you up with?'

Mario laughed. 'On the whole, no. They were perfectly nice girls that I'm sure will make some perfectly nice guys happy. Just not me.'

'But if you gave them a chance, maybe one of them would be "the one".' The wine had loosened Fleur's tongue or she wouldn't have probed further. 'If you never ask for a second date, you're never going to find out.'

Mario shook his head. 'Fool that I am, I believe in… What is it you say here? Love at first look.'

'Love at first sight.'

'That's the one. And if it doesn't happen on the first date, it never will.'

Fleur took a hefty sip. 'So you never get past a first date!'

'You are asking if I'm a thirty-five-year-old virgin?'

The hefty sip ended up spluttering across the room in a most unladylike fashion. 'No,' she said indignantly, then relented. 'Well, maybe I am. You're not, are you?'

Mario laughed. 'What a frightening thought. I'd be walking around like an unexploded time bomb. No, my lack of sexual prowess was reserved for the dates my mother set up.' He shook his head. 'I'd be at the bottom of the river with bricks tied to my feet otherwise.'

Fleur's eyes widened then she started to laugh when she realised he was teasing her.

'Actually, I'm a very good lover.'

'Modest, too.'

'No, just stating a fact. How about you?'

Now, this really was getting personal. 'I don't know,' she said indignantly. 'It's not as if I got Rory to hold up a scorecard or anything.'

Mario really laughed then. 'I'm not that crude. I meant, do you believe in love at first sight?'

'Oh.' Embarrassed, she filled up her wineglass. 'I suppose.'

'You suppose? Elaborate, come on. How was it with you and your husband?'

Suddenly Fleur did feel like holding up a scorecard and cheering. This was the first time since Rory died that another adult had spoken about him without lowering their voice. The first person that had accepted that Rory had been and still was a huge part of her life, that she wanted, no, *needed* to talk about him in a context other than his death.

'Well, for us it *was* love at first sight. He'd just moved to the area and started at my school when we first met. But when I say love, it was the sort of love that fifteen-year-olds feel. You know, he's the one! I'll simply die if he doesn't ring! It sort of grew from there. Everyone said we were too young to be serious, that it would fizzle out, but it never did. He went to the police academy, I did my nursing training, then we saved like mad and finally people stopped questioning us. We got engaged the day we put the deposit on this place.'

'You had a happy marriage obviously, from the way you talk about him.'

Fleur nodded. 'It was wonderful. Sure, we had our fights and our rough patches here and there, but it was a good marriage.' This time there was no lump in her throat as she spoke, just a sense of freedom at being able to discuss Rory so openly.

'What were your fights about?'

Fleur thought back. 'He didn't like me working in Accident and Emergency. He thought it was too rough but, considering the job he did, he didn't really have a leg to stand on.'

'And what about you, Little Miss Perfect? What did you do that annoyed Rory?'

Fleur rolled her eyes. 'I was the typical neurotic first-time mum. Didn't want to leave Alex with babysitters, constantly thought that the first sign of a sniffle meant meningitis, that sort of thing. It drove him mad.' She gave him a slightly embarrassed grin. 'Pretty much as I am now. Anyway, enough about me. If you're such a wonderful lover, how come you're not married? Haven't you ever been in love?'

Mario shrugged. 'I've thought I was a few times. I'm a romantic, I guess, but it's never worked out.'

'Why?' She felt confident, probing after revealing so much of herself.

He tapped the pager sitting on his belt. 'Usually this was the culprit.'

'How come? Normally doctors have to beat the women off with a stick.' Especially such a handsome one, Fleur wanted to add, blushing at the thoughts that were starting to take form, but instead she took refuge behind her fringe.

'Work always came first. I'd miss important family parties or get stuck late one too many times at the hospital. The only women that understood had a pager themselves and, I'm sorry to say, I didn't like it when the shoe was on the other foot.'

'You mean, when you were the one left waiting?'

Mario nodded.

'But that's so chauvinist.' Fleur argued. 'So you want your woman barefoot and pregnant in the kitchen, happily waiting for the master to return?'

Mario shook his head vehemently 'Who said anything about bare feet? A good stiletto works for me anytime.' He ducked as a cushion flew past his ear. 'Just kidding. I guess the truth is that I never really was in love. The pager,

work, whether her or me—they were all just good excuses
to end something that had already run its course. When I
look back, I'm sure I could have been fairly happy with a
couple of them, had a decent marriage, I guess. But when
I listen to how you talk about your Rory I know I am right
to wait. I, too, want a *good* marriage. My mother will just
have to wait for the bambinos.'

His glass was empty now and, ever the hostess, Fleur
leant across to fill it. His hand wandered to her thick
blonde hair, lifting the heavy fringe and pushing it off her
face. 'Why you always hide behind your hair?' His voice
was soft, questioning, his accent like a tender caress.

'Do I?' His hand held her hair back. There was nowhere
to hide now, nowhere to run. Fixing him with a bold look,
she caught her breath as his face moved towards her, his
wide, sensual mouth not aiming for her cheeks this time
but coming to rest directly on her soft full lips. Alex might
get up… That was her last coherent thought as his rough
face brushed her soft skin. And then nothing else mattered.
Just the weight of him pressing her back on to the sofa,
the scent of him drowning out all logic. His skillful hands
undoing her blouse, freeing her aching breasts from their
confines as his warm fingers moulded the heavy flesh beneath them. Everything she needed was in his kiss. It filled
her, awoke her, excited her, terrified her.

'Mario,' she gasped as his lips nuzzled her neck. It was
Mario's face pressed against hers, his black silky hair she
was running her fingers through, his body she was arching
against. It was Mario she was with and there was no place
she would rather have been.

'I want you so much,' he groaned. 'So very much.'

And she wanted him too, wanted to feel him naked
against her, wanted to explore the taut muscular body, to
trace her fingers the length of his body, to feel him inside

her. But as Fleur's eyes caught sight of her wedding photo, the image of her and Rory staring back, unblinking, she knew she couldn't go on—not here, not yet. Their bodies were so close, their emotions so attuned, he felt her sudden reluctance immediately.

'I'm sorry.' Tears were pricking at her eyes, not tears of regret but tears of frustration. With infinite tenderness he kissed her tears away.

'Never be sorry. How can you be sorry about something so beautiful?'

'Because…' She searched for the words. 'I feel as if I've let you down, led you on.'

His voice was gruff. 'You think that is why I came here? Just to make love to you?'

Fleur shook her head. 'No. It's just that I know what happened then. You wanted to, I wanted to. I just couldn't…' The words died on her lips.

'There is nothing you have to explain.' He sat up and pulled her towards him, wrapping his arms around her protectively as she sobbed into his chest. 'Of course it is too soon. And here…' she felt his hand gesture to the room '…is not the place, not for our first time. We will go somewhere special, somewhere really special where I can spoil you. And if it's still too soon, then so be it. We can talk and hold each other like we are now. You'll know when you are ready and, Fleur, I promise you this,' he said with a rueful laugh, 'I will be ready also.'

Fleur sniffed. She didn't doubt that bit for a minute— the conversation had done nothing to diminish his rather obvious ardour. 'So I'm going to get a second date?'

Mario held her tighter. 'This was never our first date. The footy was our first date, and all the other precious moments with you in between. You think I would let things go so far with such a lady on the first date? I told you before, I don't want to end up in the river.'

Fleur sat up, suddenly feeling better. 'So you liked me way back then?'

'Liked you?' he said incredulously. 'I've been crazy about you since that first day at Auskick.'

'But you said there was nothing in it, that you went out with everyone from work.'

'And I do,' he said simply. 'Don't you see that I had to play it down, or you'd never have agreed to come out with me? The people from work are just friends. You, Fleur, are different.'

Fleur gave a gurgle of laughter. 'Oh, yes, I'm a lady.'

'Not just a lady,' he said, his face moving closer. 'Every bit a woman.'

The gods that had been treating Fleur gently at work until now obviously thought she was ready for a baptism of fire, and when she walked into Resus the following morning the place seemed to explode. Mario was at his most fiery and Danny at his most irritating. For Fleur it was a case of head down and get on with it when yet another paramedic crew raced in. 'We're full,' she said apologetically as she searched in vain for an empty gurney. 'I'll have to bring a trolley over from the cubicles.'

As a trolley was located and wheeled in, the paramedic filled Fleur in on the patient's history. 'Mrs Vera Holroyd, sixty-eight years of age, collapsed at home. The GP went to do a home visit and could see her through the letterbox. He called for the ambulance.'

Fleur looked at the emaciated woman who had a coloured scarf tied around her head, tiny strands of hair escaping as they lifted her off the stretcher and onto the trolley. 'What's her history?'

'She's just finished a course of chemotherapy for ovarian cancer. Apparently there's secondaries in the liver, but that's only just been diagnosed. She's been relatively well up until now.'

'Any family?'

'She's a widow, but apparently the daughter is flying in from Queensland this morning. She's got no idea her mother is as sick as she is, of course. It's going to be a shock for her when she arrives. Anyway, I've got a neighbour's telephone number—she's going to keep an eye out for the daughter and let her know what's happened.'

'Thanks, guys.'

'No worries, Fleur.' The paramedic grinned as he neatly folded up the blanket and replaced it on his stretcher. 'I don't suppose we can beg a coffee? I hear Beryl makes a mean cappuccino.'

As Fleur took the woman's blood pressure she started to come to, moaning and thrashing around the trolley.

'It's all right, Vera, you're in hospital. I'm going to get the doctor.' Fleur said soothingly. It was obvious the woman was in some considerable pain. The junior doctors were struggling to keep up in the cubicles. Mario was shut in the interview room with some distressed relatives. Luke Richardson did his best to answer Fleur's plea to get Vera seen, but as he was juggling two extremely critical patients it was going to take a while.

'What's going on here?' Danny popped his head around the curtain as Vera screamed loudly.

'Vera Holroyd. Ovarian cancer, with liver mets, found unconscious.' Fleur spoke in low tones. 'She's come to now. I've done obs and an ECG, I'm just waiting for the doctor to see her.'

'She's in pain,' Danny stated.

'I know, but everyone's tied up. Luke's going to get to her next.'

'Well, I wouldn't hold your breath. We've just had an alert that an MVA is on the way—I've paged the trauma team. We're going to have to make some more room in here. When's the chest pain going up to CCU?'

Fleur rolled her eyes. 'CCU are supposed to ring when they're ready. I'll give them a buzz now and tell them he's on his way up, ready or not.'

'Where's Mario?'

'In with my aneurism's relatives.'

Danny gave an exasperated sigh. 'Why the hell aren't the surgeons in there with them? We need him out here.'

'They went on ahead to scrub. Danny I really need another nurse in here.'

'There isn't another nurse.' Danny answered, visibly perplexed. 'There are already a few pretty sick ones in the cubicles that really ought to be in here—*if* there was room,' he added. 'I can't spare anyone.'

Fleur understood what he was saying but it didn't mean she liked it. 'Please, see what you can do, it's getting dangerous in here. I've rung Theatre and told them how busy we are and they're going to send a nurse down directly to take the patient up.'

'Good. I'll ring CCU and get them to do the same while you set up for the MVA.' He looked over to the trolley as Vera let out a guttural scream. 'Get her seen, Fleur, for heaven's sake. She needs some pain control.'

Easier said than done. Luke's patient suddenly deteriorated and Fleur had to assist Felicity in the resuscitation while simultaneously setting up for the MVA and attempting to soothe Vera. Thankfully the theatre and CCU nurses arrived speedily, which probably had more to do with Danny's menacing mood than anything else.

There was the tiniest breathing space as two of the patients exited the area, and Fleur was able to concentrate on helping Felicity. But as the wailing of sirens filtered through and blue lights flashed past the darkened windows, the momentum soon lifted.

One look at the new patient and Fleur knew he was in big trouble. 'Danny, I need more help in here!' she called out to the corridor. 'Now!'

The trauma team, consisting of the orthopaedic registrar and an anaesthetist, arrived just as the patient was lifted over. Mario rushed in moments later, somewhat breathless.

'What's the story?'

As the paramedics relayed the grim history Danny made a brief appearance. 'I need more nurses,' Fleur said urgently. 'Felicity's still stuck with Mr Richardson.'

'Has Mrs Holroyd been seen?'

Danny was really starting to test her patience now. 'You mean since the last time you popped your head in?' Opening a chest tube, Fleur never missed a beat as she assisted the doctors. 'I need some help now, Danny. If you can't spare anyone, how about *you* put an apron on?'

Pointedly ignoring her, Danny addressed Mario. 'Can you see Mrs Holroyd on the next trolley?'

Mario pulled the stethoscope out of his ears. 'Actually, I'm a bit tied up at the moment.'

The sarcasm was wasted on Danny. 'The trauma team will have to deal with this. I want Mrs Holroyd seen, she's in pain.'

Fleur bit her lip, half expecting a string of Italian expletives to fill the air, but surprisingly the only dramatic gesture was Mario tearing off his gloves in a rather exasperated fashion. 'Fine.'

As the morning whizzed on at a frenzied pace, Fleur had little time to dwell on Danny's black mood. But finally, when Resus, if not empty exactly, was a lot calmer and the chance for a coffee was simply too good to ignore, she sank gratefully into a chair, wishing the coffee-cup she was drinking from was bottomless.

'What gives with your boss?'

Fleur grinned as Mario entered. 'Oh, so it's Danny when he's being nice and my boss when he's in a strop.' She watched as Mario sat down, stretching his long legs out in front of him. 'I don't know what his problem is,' she admitted. 'I know it's been really busy this morning, but I've seen it a lot worse and normally nothing much ruffles Danny. That's what makes him such a good emergency nurse.'

'Does he know Vera?'

Fleur screwed up her forehead 'Oh, Mrs Holroyd. No, at least I don't think so. I know it was upsetting, and I wanted her to be seen as quickly as possible. It's horrible when someone's in pain, but you saw what it was like—sometimes it's simply not possible. Danny knows that better than anyone. How is she doing?'

Mario shook his head. 'I've spoken with the surgeons. They did a CT and the cancer's everywhere and on top of that she's now in heart failure. All we can do is keep her comfortable, poor woman.'

'Her daughter's flying in. Do you think she'll get here in time?'

Mario shrugged. 'Hard to say. I rang the neighbour, Marjory, and explained things. She's a lovely woman, and she's going to meet the daughter at the airport and drive her straight here. Hopefully we can get Vera up to a ward soon.'

Fleur drank the last of her coffee. 'I doubt it. There's no beds anywhere. How's her pain now?'

'Controlled, but let me know if she needs anything

stronger. I don't think this is the time to be holding back on pain control. You won't be looking after her now, though. She's been moved out of Resus to cubicle four.'

'Fleur?' Danny's bark came over the intercom.

'On my way,' Fleur answered, pressing the talk-back button.

'Already,' Mario grumbled. 'Tell him you're tied up.'

Fleur gave Mario the tiniest wink as she made to go. 'In your dreams, Mr Ruffini.'

'Well, now you mention it…' Catching her wrist as she brushed past, Mario spun her around. 'I hear you're going to be at a loose end next Friday night, so how about you let me spoil you for once?'

'What did you have in mind?'

'Somewhere special, romantic, just us…'

'Fleur!' Danny sounded as if he was set to come and fetch her himself!

'We'll talk about it later. I really have to go now.'

As she walked back to Resus she passed Wendy coming out of the interview room. The fact that the surgeons were talking to relatives so soon could only mean the patient hadn't made it. Catching a glimpse of Wendy's reddened eyes, Fleur gave a small smile of greeting, 'How are you doing, Wendy?'

'I'm fine,' Wendy said stiffly, then flashed a smile. 'Honestly, Fleur. Look, I'm sorry about yesterday; I was just letting off a bit of steam. You know what it's like.'

Fleur did know what it was like. Hadn't she, too, flashed that reassuring smile and said she was fine when fine was the last thing she'd been? What was it with this place? They were all educated, sensitive people, supposedly this great 'team' that supported each other. So why did it sometimes feel so lonely?

Collecting her bag, Fleur said her goodbyes and made

her way through section A. Hesitating outside cubicle 4, she pulled the curtain and saw Danny and Lucy checking Mrs Holroyd's ID band before administering more morphine. 'How's she doing?'

'Holding on for her daughter to get here, I think.' There was something in Danny's voice Fleur couldn't read, and she watched as he gently stroked the frail hand he held beneath his. 'I'd better get back out, the place is steaming out there. It would have been nice if we could have got her up to a ward. It seems a shame for her to be down here on her own.'

Fleur put her bag down on the floor. 'You get on, Danny. I'll sit with her.'

Danny looked up. 'But you're finished for the day.'

Fleur gave a small smile. 'You don't stop being a nurse just because your shift's ended. Go on, Danny. I'll stay.'

With the curtain drawn, Fleur made herself as comfortable as she could on the hard, cold seat. Taking Vera's hands, she practised not what she had learned in nursing school but what came instinctively. Talking gently, her fingers occasionally stroking the lined brow, Fleur did what nurses sometimes did: made Vera's final journey just that little bit easier and a little less lonely.

And later, as she made her way out into the bright afternoon sun, rushing to pick the boys up from school, Fleur finally knew that she'd been right to come back. It might be one helluva job, but it was hers.

CHAPTER EIGHT

FLEUR wasn't sure who was more excited—Alex, at the prospect of his long-awaited first sleep-over, or herself, at the prospect of a night alone with Mario. Over and over he'd reassured her that he didn't expect anything she wasn't ready to give. He just wanted a night away on neutral territory, a chance to be themselves without the constant interruptions and inevitable distractions that came hand in hand when you tried to conduct a relationship in a houseful of memories with an inquisitive seven-year-old *in situ*.

'Where are you rushing off to?' Kathy asked as Fleur flew into the changing room at the end of her shift on Friday, anxious to cram in her hairdresser's appointment before the school run.

'Nowhere special. I just want to get a few things done before I pick up the boys. How was Alex this morning?'

Kathy laughed as she pulled off her jeans and T-shirt and slipped on her uniform. 'Thoroughly over-excited. Mind you, Ben's just as bad. I pity Ricky's parents—and Mario. They won't be getting much sleep tonight. Hey, maybe we should offer Mario some refuge. He could come on a girls' night out with us.'

Fleur suddenly took great interest in fiddling with her hair in the mirror.

'How about it, Fleur? We could go down to the local pub have a bit of a laugh. It's not every night we both get a babysitter at the same time.'

'Maybe some other time,' Fleur replied lightly, glad she

had her back to Kathy as her face turned puce. The only trouble was, she'd forgotten about her reflection!

'Fleur Hadley, I do believe you're blushing.'

'I am not.' Fleur said indignantly.

'Oh, yes, you are! You're positively beetroot. You always were a useless liar. Come on, you can tell me. What are you up to?'

Fleur's silence only confirmed Kathy's suspicions. 'You've already got a date, haven't you?'

Fleur put her finger up to her lips. 'Shh, Kathy, please,' she said urgently.

'You dark horse.' Kathy grinned. 'How come you didn't tell me? Oh, come on, Fleur, who with? And stop shushing me. Nobody's here and anyway why would they care?' As the penny dropped, Kathy's eyes widened like two saucers. 'Unless, of course, it's a date with Mario Ruffini!' She let out a squeal of excitement as Fleur begged her to be quiet.

'Kathy, it's no big deal, really.'

But Kathy wasn't going to let up. 'Good for you, Fleur. He's gorgeous. I'm even the tiniest smidgen jealous.'

'Well, there's no need to be. We're just going out for a drink, it's hardly anything to get worked up about.'

'Fleur, this is *me* you're talking to. When was the last time you *just* went out for a drink?'

'All right, all right,' Fleur relented. 'Maybe it is a big deal, but you have to promise not to say anything. I mean it, Kathy. I'd die if this got out, it's just way too early.'

'My lips are sealed.' Kathy grinned. 'So long as you fill me in properly tomorrow, and I mean properly. I'll bring the wine, you provide the chocolate.'

'And you won't breathe a word?'

'I promise.'

Picking up her bag, Fleur reluctantly opened the door.

Making Kathy cross her heart was probably taking things a bit far, but she suddenly felt exposed.

'Kathy?'

'I promised, didn't I?' Kathy said, not looking up as she tied up her shoelaces.

'That's not what I was going to ask. I guess I'm just going to have to trust you on that one.'

'What then?'

'Is there any chance I could borrow your grey shoes— you know, the suede ones?'

Kathy picked up a hairbrush and laughingly threw it at the door. 'Get out of here, you scarlet woman, and let the rest of us do some work!'

Shaved, plucked, oiled and scented to within an inch of her life, Fleur threw a long jacket over her dress and dropped off Alex.

'Thanks, Teresa. If there's any problem, anything at all, please, ring me.' Fleur's colour deepened as she continued, 'I'm having a bit of trouble with my telephone, so here's my mobile number. I'll have it on all night so don't hesitate to ring.'

'Sure, no worries.' Fleur was positive Teresa gave her a brief wink. 'Say goodnight to your mum, Alex. I'm sure she's got things to do.' Kissing Alex, still blushing furiously, Fleur made her way down the garden path. Kathy knew, Teresa knew. Heaven knew who else was in on it by now. They might as well set up a live telecast at this rate!

Back home Fleur admired her newly styled hair, her thick blonde locks for once straightened and twisted gently into a chic French roll. Her fringe was glossy and smooth, falling seductively over one eye. All that was needed was a touch more lipstick and then she squeezed her feet into the impossibly slim grey heels Kathy had happily lent her. Finally she was ready, well, almost. Walking over to the mantelpiece, she stood a moment.

'I wish I knew how you felt about this, Rory.' Looking down at her trembling hands, she focussed on her rings. Here's the bit the magazines don't tell you, Fleur thought. Why wasn't there some sort of etiquette manual for widows that told you what to do on nights like this? How could she sleep with another man while she still wore Rory's rings? Yet how could she bear to take them off? And if she did take the rings off, what then? What was she supposed to do with them? Toss them into her jewellery box, put them on the other hand? Fleur looked back at the picture, again searching Rory's features for some clue, some sign, anything that would indicate his take on all this.

'You know I love you, Rory. I always will.' With a shaking hand Fleur pulled at her rings, but as they reached her knuckle with a sob of frustration she rammed them back down her finger. She just wasn't ready to leave that part of her behind, at least not yet.

'Now will you tell me where we're going?'

Mario had taken the beach road and they were obviously heading towards the city. Daylight saving had just started and Melbourne was making the most of it, the beach dotted with couples, children and groups of teenagers, all enjoying the long days. The pavement cafés and pub gardens that whizzed past as Mario put his foot down were all fit to burst with women, gorgeous in pretty short dresses and guys in shorts or suits, taking a moment to enjoy the end of a long week and the start of the weekend. To Fleur's utter surprise, the nerves that had had her in a spin all week had abated almost as soon as Mario had arrived at

her door. Now all she felt was excited, carefree and looking forward to the evening ahead.

'I love this city.' Mario took his eyes off the road for a
second and grinned at her. 'Everyone here knows how to
have a good time. Beautiful restaurants, cafés, bars, the
beach.'

'You'd have all that in Rome, though—I mean, except
the beach.'

Mario nodded. 'Of course. I wasn't comparing—they
are both beautiful cities. I was just saying how much I am
enjoying my time here.'

Fleur leant back in her seat, trying not to let what he'd
said niggle at her. 'My time here.' She'd known from the
day they'd met that he was only there for a year, and for
the last couple of weeks the prospect that he would one
day be gone had been all too often invading her thoughts.
But she wasn't going to let it spoil tonight. It was just too
big a thought to deal with, like an impossible conundrum
put before her.

How could she let herself fall in love, let him into her
and Alex's life, only to lose him. Yet how could she not?
He had breezed into her life and in his own unique way
given her a glimpse of what life could be like again. How
could she turn her back on all the joy he brought, based
on the premise that six months down the track she was
maybe going to get hurt? For now it was time to simply
get to know each other. The hows and whys would just
have to be dealt with later.

'Have you guessed yet?'

As the car turned into Spring Street Fleur let out a moan
of delight. 'The Windsor?' she gasped as the car glided
into the reserved spot, the doorman rushing to assist. 'I've
always wanted to stay here.'

'Me, too. I read about it in my Australian guidebook.

Apparently it's almost mandatory—take a tram ride, eat at Chinatown, footy at the MCG, a show at The Arts Centre…'

'Well, I'm glad I'm helping you tick something off your list,' Fleur said indignantly.

'If you'd let me finish, I was about to add afternoon tea at the Windsor—it's supposed to be wonderful. I thought we might take it up a notch. What I have planned for tonight was never on my itinerary. Let's just enjoy it, huh?'

How could she not? As the car door was opened and she stepped out, Mario took her arm and they walked together up the steps into the magnificent foyer. Fleur stood gazing at the huge floral display and the vast Milton tiled staircase as Mario dealt with the formalities.

'I've booked dinner for eight—I thought that might give us a chance to have a quick drink to unwind. Is that all right with you?'

She knew she should have been nervous, but as the bell-boy deposited their bags on the vast bed and discreetly left, all Fleur could do was gasp in wonder as she looked around the opulent suite at the tasteful rosewood furniture, the huge open fireplace and heavy silk drapes. Even the bathroom was divine, boasting a deep claw-foot bath that seemed to beg Fleur to sink into it.

'*Magnifico*,' Mario murmured, gazing out the window overlooking Treasury Gardens. Turning, he expertly opened the bottle of champagne that awaited them. 'But all this would mean nothing if you weren't here with me.'

'Flatterer.' Fleur grinned, holding out her hand for the glass of champagne he was offering.

As their glasses chinked she caught his eye. 'To us,' he murmured softly.

Holding his gaze, she wrapped her fingers tightly along

the long stem of the crystal glass. 'To us.' Her voice was almost a whisper, the cool champagne a heady contrast to the heat sizzling between them. A drink to unwind was the misnomer of the century, judging by the crackling tension that hummed in the room. Taking the glass from her hand, he placed it on the table before slowly, deliberately he moved towards her, his lips drawn to hers as if by some unseen force. She could taste the champagne as his cool tongue met hers, feel the heat between them as they pressed their aching groins towards each other, his arousal straining against her flimsy dress.

But she needed more.

He felt it, too.

As they fell down onto the chaise longue he could feel his manhood against her, and she instinctively lifted her leg, wrapping it around his hips, pulling him ever tighter to her. But just as being wined and dined was becoming a distinct impossibility the shrill sound of her mobile had Fleur rummaging for her bag.

'It might be about Alex,' she explained as she desperately tried to locate the phone.

Mario coughed and stood up, subtly rearranging his attire as Fleur mumbled 'yes' and 'no' into the mobile. Finally she concluded the call and with a wail of frustration hurled the beastly thing onto the bed.

'Alex?' Mario asked.

'No,' she snapped in frustration. Starting to laugh a touch hysterically, she picked up her glass of champagne as Mario joined her, a bemused grin on his face.

'Then who?'

'Just this blessed woman from the school uniform shop who keeps hounding me! Aren't I allowed to have a life?'

Dinner was divine. Fleur felt impossibly spoilt as waiters unfolded huge white napkins in her lap and filled her glass. They lingered over their aperitifs, enjoying the elegance of the grand dining room, groaning with the weight of indecision as they pondered the menu. But as the evening progressed, and their plates were cleared and desserts finally chosen, Fleur looked up. The bluest, kindest eyes were smiling at her, adoring her, and under his steady gaze Fleur truly felt beautiful. The food, the service, the grandeur of the surroundings had all played their part but it was this sensual, thoughtful man that had the lead role. And finally, like the mist clearing on a mirror, she saw him as if for the first time, saw how good life could be with a man like Mario at her side, if only she let him in.

'You said to tell you when I was ready.'

Mario reached over and took her hand, his searching eyes never leaving her face for a second.

'I'm ready, Mario,' Fleur said softly.

'You're sure?'

This time she didn't duck behind her fringe, there was nothing to fear now. 'I'm sure, Mario.' Removing her napkin from her lap, she placed it on the table and slowly, purposefully stood up.

As the waiter approached, Mario's eyes widened in surprise. 'You mean now? You're ready now, this minute? But dessert....' His voice trailed off as two delectable white chocolate mousses were placed on the table.

'Is everything all right, sir?'

Fleur flashed a wicked grin as she watched him flounder for the first time.

'Everything is perfect,' Mario replied, clearing his throat as he rose and joined her. 'But we have decided to take dessert in our room. Perhaps I could ring down when we are ready.'

The waiter didn't bat an eyelid, only magnifying Mario's nervousness. 'Certainly, sir.'

Leaving the grand dining room and crossing the hotel foyer, Fleur let out a peal of laughter as Mario grabbed her hand. 'Do you think he knew?'

'Knew what?' Fleur giggled. 'That a huge wave of lust suddenly overcame me? Of course he knew!'

As the lift inched its way up to the third floor he kissed her passionately, reluctantly stopping as the doors opened. Only when they were safely inside the suite, when his hot kisses were stealing down her neck, his hands unzipping the crimson chiffon, only then did Fleur have a moment of panic. As her dress fluttered to the ground and she felt his hungry eyes searching her body as he unclasped her bra, images of lithe Italian beauties, olive-skinned, toned and gorgeous, flashed through her mind. But as his fingers gently touched the pale pink swell of her nipples, as a guttural moan of desire escaped from his lips, she saw the desire blazing in his eyes and Fleur felt as sexy and as beautiful as she'd ever felt in her life.

Tentatively at first, she undid the buttons of his shirt and wrestled with the heavy weight of his belt buckle. But as she glimpsed the dark skin, glimpsed the jet hair that fanned over his chest, her nerves were forgotten as the need to see him, to hold him surpassed all else. And finally when there was nothing between them except the white heat that radiated from their bodies, Fleur ran her eyes over every inch of him, and he was as wondrous as she'd imagined—only more somehow. The ebon hair that matted his chest, thick yet soft, his nipples as dark as mahogany stiffening under her touch. And as her fingers crept downwards she felt giddy with longing as she encountered the coarse thicket of hair, her fingers tracing the heated length of his manhood.

'My beautiful Fleur.' His voice was like a silken kiss. Gently he laid her on the huge bed, his hand creeping slowly along the soft marshmallow of her thigh. She caught her breath as he met the damp sweet velvet, gasping with pleasure as she let him explore her, revelling under his masterful touch. As he slowly entered her, Fleur felt a piercing stab of pleasure as if she were making love for the first time. And afterwards, as she lay in his arms and he held her close, whispering words that she had never heard before yet understood perfectly, Fleur revelled in the significance of what had just taken place. It had been the first time after all—it had been *their* first time.

'What are you thinking, *bella*?'

Fleur nestled deeper into Mario's arms, a tiny shiver whispering over her as the rosy flush of love receded. 'How nice I was feeling. How nice *you* make me feel.' She planted a tiny kiss on his chest. 'How I really fancy that chocolate mousse.'

'Fleur.' Feigning hurt, he sat up. 'How can you think of food at a time like this?'

Fleur laughed, 'That mousse really did look delicious and if you knew my penchant for chocolate you'd be eternally flattered that I didn't stay downstairs for dessert.'

'So, was I worth skipping the mousse for?' One hand was twining her blonde hair around his fingers while the other ran lazily along her the curve of her hips.

'Who said anything about skipping it?' Reaching over, Fleur grabbed the telephone but Mario was too quick for her. Laughing, he executed a perfect tackle. Forcing a giggling Fleur onto her back, he straddled her between his muscular legs. 'If you're expecting me to escort you downstairs for breakfast tomorrow, you'll at least have the decency to wait a bit longer before ringing. We Italians have a reputation to uphold!'

*   *   *

Awakening in Mario's arms, Fleur lay for a moment, her eyes drifting around the sumptuous room, the scent of jonquils and freesias filled the air, and she surveyed the rumpled sheets, the empty dessert dishes. Reliving their lovemaking, she felt a shudder of delight go through her.

What she had expected from their first time together she wasn't sure—some awkwardness perhaps, some hesitation. Never had she dared hope it might be so rapturous so soon. That whilst revelling in the unfamiliarity of each other's bodies, they would have been so instinctively attuned to each other's needs, desires... Turning slightly, she gazed at him for a while, his dark eyelashes fanning over his cheeks, the haughty, straight nose, the rough morning shadow smudging his strong jawline, and she knew then that she was the luckiest woman in the world.

Allowing herself the tiniest indulgent daydream, she imagined what it would be like to wake up beside him every morning, to see the sapphire of his eyes as he awoke, to be the recipient of that beautiful smile, to succumb to his love-making over and over. And though it was a wonderful daydream and she could have happily lain there gazing at him for hours, she also knew their time was precious, that the clock was ticking down on their stolen hours together.

'Mario,' she whispered, her lips moving towards him to awaken him with a kiss. He stirred beneath her, his lips warm and soft, a contrast to his arousal as she inched in closer. After the urgency of the previous night, their lovemaking was deliciously slow, a tender confirmation of the love they shared, another glimpse of paradise.

By the time they surfaced for breakfast they practically had the dining room to themselves, falling like starving dingoes on the delicious food spread before them.

Full fit to burst, Fleur still gave in to temptation and,

spreading blackberry jam over a warm croissant, she felt him staring at her. 'What are you thinking?'

It was nice to be able to answer honestly. 'That I never want this morning to end.'

'You've had a good time, then?'

Fleur nodded. 'It's been wonderful, you've been wonderful. I feel thoroughly spoilt.'

'Which was exactly what I intended. You deserve to be spoilt.'

Fleur didn't answer. Taking a sip of her coffee, she replaced the cup in the saucer. 'Mario, why me?'

He looked at her, nonplussed. 'What do you mean?'

'I mean, you could have any woman you want. Why on earth would you choose me? I'm hardly traffic-stoppingly gorgeous, and it's not as if I'm footloose and fancy-free.'

'You mean Alex?'

Fleur nodded. The last thing she wanted to do was spoil their time together, but Alex, her situation—these were things that couldn't be ignored. She didn't have the luxury of following her heart and to hell with the consequences. She was a mother first, she needed to know where she stood.

Mario stood up, offering her his hand. 'Come, let's walk.'

They wandered out into Spring Street, pausing as a tram clattered past and walking hand in hand past Parliament House and the short distance to Treasury Gardens. Spring was all around, the morning warm, the gardens ablaze with colour.

Beneath a huge palm tree they stopped. Turning her to face him, Mario gently took Fleur's face in his hands, faltering slightly with his English as he spoke. 'You ask why you? Now I will ask the same. Why me?'

'But I asked first,' she argued, trying to free her face

from his hands. But he held her firmly, forcing her to look at him. 'All right then,' she said, swallowing nervously. 'I'll tell you. How could I not want you, how could any woman not?' She was almost angry as she continued. 'You're good-looking, clever, kind, funny. Anyway, you must know all of this, Mario. I'm sure lots of your girl-friends have told you already. Why make me say it?

'So come on. Now it's your turn. Why me, Mario? Why would you choose me with my moods, my permanent state of anxiety…' Fleur looked down and screwed her eyes closed as she continued, but still his hands held her face. 'My stretch marks, my seven-year-old son? You know me well enough to know I'm not interested in a casual fling!' There. She'd finally said it! Fleur held her eyes closed, waiting for his response, her breathing coming out rapidly.

She felt his warm breath on her cheeks, small butterfly kisses chasing the salty tears away.

'Hey, hey.' His hands left her face as he wrapped his arms fiercely around her. 'It's *because* of all those things that I adore you. How about volatile and passionate instead of moody and anxious? How about the softest, smoothest body that turns me to water, and how about the fact that you *do* have a seven-year-old son that you love and put before everyone, even yourself? Can you see now how easy it is for me to adore you? And, Fleur, the very last thing I want from you is a casual relationship. I swear to you, there's nothing casual about the way I'm feeling.'

She leant against him, feeling the tension seep from her body, bathed in the bliss of his words. 'But how—?'

'Fleur.' He let her go. Standing back slightly, he took her hands. 'What do you want me to say here? Cannot what we have shared last night be enough for now? I adore you, Fleur. I would never hurt you in a million years…'

But 'adore' wasn't the same word as 'love'.

'You live in Italy, Mario. I think being hurt is a bit closer than a million years away.'

The sun was shining directly in his eyes, making him squint slightly. 'And you have a son. We owe it to him not to go making rash promises. We need time, Fleur, time to get to know each other some more, time to see where this is leading. Only then can we work out the answers.'

They wandered back hand in hand and, after making their way back to their room, set about packing their overnight bags. Fleur felt like a child when the Christmas tree was being put away. She didn't want it to be over, she wanted it to carry on for ever. 'How many more sleeps?' she asked quietly, smiling as Mario caught her eyes. 'It's what Alex always says,' she explained. 'How many more sleeps till my birthday, how many more sleeps till Christmas?'

He came around and held her as she continued, 'I was just wondering how many more sleeps until we'll be together again—properly, I mean.'

'There's not a school camp coming up?' he asked hopefully.

Fleur shook her head. 'Not till next year.'

'How about Kathy? Maybe she could have him for a night?'

Fleur stiffened slightly at the mention of Kathy's name. 'She knows about us, well, sort of. I didn't tell her—she kind of guessed.'

Mario didn't seem remotely fazed by the possibility of them being a bit more public. It was Fleur who had that problem. 'Good,' he said lightly. 'Then I'm sure she'll babysit one night.'

But Fleur shook her head. 'Look, she might know a bit of what's going on, but I'd rather we played it down. I really don't want anyone else at work getting wind of this.'

Mario looked at her, puzzled. 'I can understand you holding back on telling Alex, but work—'

'Please, Mario, it's just too soon. People might…' Her voice trailed off but Mario insisted she finish what she was saying.

'Might what?'

Fleur searched around her head for the right words. 'Might judge me. They might think that it's too soon.'

'Too soon for what, Fleur? Too soon to be happy?'

She couldn't answer. How could she expect him to understand when she didn't really understand herself?

'All right,' Mario relented. 'If you want to keep it quiet at work for now, that's fine, but I'm not carrying on like some fugitive in front of Teresa.'

Fleur managed a watery smile. 'It's OK, Mario, I guessed already that she knew.' Curiosity got the better of her. 'What did she say?'

'Oh, she was horrified. Said how terrible it was that you were out gallivanting off to the Windsor with me when you should be home where you belong, worrying whether Alex was having a good night.'

It took a second to register that he was joking.

'She wants to meet you, you know, away from the school gates. There's an engagement party next Saturday for Marco's younger sister and she wondered if you'd like to come.'

'But it's Alex's birthday—he's having a tenpin-bowling party.'

'In the afternoon,' Mario pointed out. 'Alex can come to the engagement party, too. There'll be loads of children there, he'll have a great time.'

Fleur felt a bubble of panic rising within her. 'It's a bit soon to be meeting the family, Mario.'

He laughed at that. 'On the contrary, given what happened last night, by Italian standards we've left it rather late. Anyway,' he said, grinning, 'apart from Teresa, who you've already met, the Ruffini contingent there will hardly be heavyweights—just a few cousins and second cousins, great-aunts, that sort of thing.'

'Will there be lots of them?' she asked nervously.

'Hundreds. The Ruffinis are a huge family. We're everywhere.'

Fleur chewed her lip 'Will you be upset if we don't go?'

'Oh, I'll survive,' he said heavily, but there was a twinkle in his eye as he continued, 'Of course, as a single man I'll be seated next to some dark-haired beauty who I'll be expected to dance with all night under the hopeful eyes of a hundred Italians.' He grinned as Fleur pursed her lips. 'All waiting for the lights to dim and the music to slow down. All hoping for an excuse to fly to Italy next year for the Ruffini marriage of the century...'

Fleur found she was grinning, too. 'OK, OK, I'll come.'

He dropped her off at home so she could arrive at Teresa's without raising any eyebrows, from Alex at least. As she walked through the front door Fleur braced herself, expecting what, she didn't know—perhaps a penance for her night with Mario. But the house was exactly as she'd left it, the scent of her liberally sprayed perfume still hanging in the air from the night before, the half-drunk glass of wine to steady her nerves still on the coffee-table and her wedding picture in its place. Rory's eyes were still smiling, the clock was still ticking and the world was moving right along as usual.

CHAPTER NINE

'OK, MARIO, where did you want to start?' Luke peered around the table at the gathered staff. The weekly meeting of senior nursing staff and doctors was more of a chore than anything else. It was supposed to be a chance to discuss any interesting or difficult cases that had come up, an opportunity to air any grievances and work out how, or if, things could be done better. In reality it generally lasted no more than twenty minutes, with everyone rushing off for lunch. However, today, just as the meeting got under way, a loud rap on the door caused everyone to turn.

'Pizza.'

'I think you've got the wrong room,' Fleur said quickly. 'Perhaps ask at reception.' But Mario stood up.

'No, they are for here. I ordered them.' Paying the delivery boy, he unburdened him of several red boxes and deposited them on the table. 'I thought if we had lunch here, it might give us more of a chance to talk.'

At first everyone just sat there, no one wanting to be the first to help themselves, but as the gorgeous smell of fresh-baked pizza filled the room Danny succumbed first as Mario started going through the cases. Initially the meeting carried on pretty much as it always did, with no one, bar Mario, contributing much other than an occasional groan or wry smile. But when Mario brought up young Archie Levitski the mood shifted as Mario started speaking passionately.

'My younger brother, Silvio, was badly bitten by a dog when he was a baby. Now, I know it was many years ago

124

and in another country but seeing Archie brought a lot of memories back—my mother's guilt, my father's anger. It's a scenario that is played out daily the world over. I feel that we as a unit should try to change things.'

Danny laughed. 'How? Archie Levitski was on every news bulletin and current affairs show for at least a week after the event, yet I for one haven't noticed a decline in dogbites coming through the department. If the pictures of his injuries weren't enough to wake up the public, I don't see what difference we can make.'

The rest of the staff murmured their agreement and carried on with their pizza, but Mario was far from finished. 'I don't for one minute think we can change the world, but I most certainly believe we can make a difference. It may sound like a cliché, but if we can stop just one child suffering the injuries Archie sustained, I think it will be more than worth it.'

'You still haven't told us how,' Danny responded, unmoved.

'If you gave me a moment to speak, perhaps I might be able to.' Danny shrugged and carried on eating as Mario continued. 'I have spoken with Mrs Levitski and together we are considering going around local kindergartens and schools to talk both with the children and hopefully the parents. I have already discussed this with the local police and RSPCA and they, too, are interested in coming along.'

'It's not a bad idea, actually,' Luke said, looking up from his notes. 'Mrs Levitski might just make a couple of parents sit up and take notice. How's the child doing now?'

Mario grinned. 'Very well, I'm happy to say. He has been released from hospital and Mr Hassed did a marvellous job on his injuries. Of course, the psychological damage that has been caused will take longer to heal but his mother is a good and patient woman. I'm sure he will do well.

'So how about it, guys? I can't do this on my own. The odd meeting, yes, but with the agenda Mrs Levitski seems to have planned, I'm going to need a lot of help if we're going to get this off the ground.'

'I don't mind going along now and then,' Fleur offered, and Mario nodded appreciatively.

'Sounds good,' Kathy agreed, as everyone started to put their hands up. 'Perhaps you could do a talk at Ben's school.'

The rest of the patients were rather more straightforward, although waiting times in the department seemed, as always, to be the main bone of contention. The meeting carried on pretty much as it always did until they came to the last patient.

'I would now like to discuss the treatment Mrs Vera Holroyd received in the department.'

Fleur furrowed her brow and looked down at her list as Mario spoke. What did he want to discuss? As sad as it had been, it really had been fairly uneventful in terms of the department.

'Danny, I believe you were upset that she waited so long without being given any pain control?'

'Look…' Danny shifted in his seat uncomfortably. 'It was no one's fault. It *was* exceptionally busy that morning and in hindsight she really didn't wait that long.'

'But it seemed a long while at the time?' Mario was staring directly at Danny, and the piece of pizza that had been working its way towards Fleur's mouth, stopped as she picked up on the sudden tension in the room.

'Yes,' Danny said, lowering his eyes and pretending to read his notes. 'But, as I said, in reality it was only a matter of ten minutes or so.'

'You were also, if I remember rightly, annoyed that we couldn't get Mrs Holroyd moved up to a ward?'

'Yes again,' Danny said slowly, choosing his words carefully. 'But it was the same old story—no beds.'

'Which, as we all know, is very frustrating when you have a woman dying and no ward to send her to.' His eyes never left Danny, who had assumed a relaxed pose now as he shrugged dismissively.

'It happens here every day. It's no big deal.'

'On the contrary.' Mario spoke sharply. 'A woman was in pain and no doctor was available to attend to her, coupled with the fact she had to die down here in Accident and Emergency when she should have been in a comfortable bed.'

'Look,' Danny said heavily. 'I know now there was nothing that could have been done differently. It's just that…' He looked down again, taking a couple of breaths before continuing, 'My partner's mother died last year from ovarian cancer. The plan had been for her to die at home surrounded by the people she loved, but it didn't work out like that. Geoff panicked at the last minute and we ended up calling an ambulance, and she died soon after in Casualty, on a hard trolley and in pain. Mrs Holroyd was just a bit too close to home.'

'She wasn't in any pain when she died,' Fleur said quickly. 'I stayed with her and her daughter, and in the end Vera, I mean Mrs Holroyd, was made very comfortable.'

'I know,' Danny admitted. 'It just upset me at the time. When Geoff's mother died, we were in a different accident department on the other side of town, and there was nothing I could do to help. I felt so useless. I mean, what sort of a nurse am I if I can't even help someone I'm close to? I still don't think he's really forgiven me.'

Mario cleared his throat. 'Perhaps in circumstances such as these we could consider opening up the overnight stay ward, even if it means having to use an agency nurse. I know it might put an extra strain on the budget but, hey, what's new about that?'

The floodgates opened then. It was as if Danny's admission had paved the way for the rest of the staff to open up a bit. To admit that it wasn't always easy. Wendy confessed she was having trouble with her marriage. She knew she was a good doctor and a great surgeon but right here, right now she could really use a bit of extra support. Luke even admitted that his middle son was suffering from depression and every overdose that came in hit him hard. The pizza had long since gone and they were munching their way through a packet of biscuits when Mario finally concluded the meeting.

'Well, hopefully we've all learned a lot today, not just about the department but about each other. It goes without saying, of course, that what was said in here stays in here. Same time next week, guys.'

Danny stood up, slightly pink at having revealed so much. 'Hey, Mario,' he called across the table. 'Next time no anchovies, please.'

'How did you do that?' Fleur stood, open-mouthed, after they'd all gone.

Mario stapled some papers together and stood up. 'Amazing what a pizza will do, huh? I still can't believe it myself.'

'I know what you mean,' Fleur agreed, her voice serious. 'All of us going about our business, never opening up, and underneath there's all that pain. Just look at Luke and Wendy…'

Mario laughed as he stuffed the papers into his briefcase. 'Not that,' he said in a theatrical whisper. 'I just

never had the faintest idea Danny was gay!' And ducking
the playful thump Fleur threw at him, they made their way
back into the department.

Almost from that moment, the department seemed to
lift. It seemed strange that something as simple as sharing
a meal and a few private thoughts could have had such a
dramatic effect, but suddenly there seemed to be more
comradeship between the staff. You couldn't shed the worries of the outside world when you pulled on your uniform,
but having your colleagues looking out for you, knowing
what buttons to avoid being pushed, made it easier all
round.

At any given time one of the staff that attended the
weekly meetings was on duty so as far as possible the
serious overdoses were discreetly given to Mario rather
than Luke. When the going got tough with relatives Fleur,
or whoever else was on, might step in a bit sooner to save
Wendy the anguish. And as for Danny, realising that he'd
lost his confidence a bit, realising he was questioning his
vocation, made it a bit easier to drag him out of his office.
They weren't avoiding their own individual issues, as Fleur
had when she'd first came back. Instead, they were simply
sharing the load a bit more, making it easier to get through
a shift on the front line.

Mario had also managed to work his magic on the home
front. Alex, it seemed, adored him as much as Fleur, if
that was at all possible, and when he arrived at Alex's
tenpin-bowling party, carrying a terribly wrapped football,
Alex was unable to contain his delight, jumping up and
down as he introduced Mario to all his friends.

Fleur was only marginally less contained when she saw
him. 'Thank goodness you're here. I've never known such
a rabble, and Kathy vanished twenty minutes ago on the

premise of rustling up some coffee. How the hell am I supposed to get this lot bowling?'

'Leave it to me,' Mario said, rolling up his sleeves.

'But you need to get bowling shoes. What size are you?'

'I've got my own,' he said, producing a pair out of a carrier bag. 'What is wrong?' he asked as Kathy, returning with two coffees, joined Fleur in hysterical laughter. 'Why do you both laugh?'

'I'm sorry,' Fleur gulped, trying to contain her giggles. 'It's just not many men I know carry their own...' She doubled over as Kathy started to roar. 'Their own bowling shoes!'

'Well,' he said haughtily, 'we'll see who's laughing in half an hour!' And, turning smartly on his red leather heel, he made his way over to the excited group, leaving Kathy and Fleur to giggle over their coffee as he marshalled the boys together and in no time had a semblance of a bowling match taking place.

'You've got to hand it to him.' Kathy grinned as they sat back. 'He's turned what could have been the afternoon from hell into a very pleasant chance for a gossip.'

'Leave it, Kathy,' Fleur warned lightly.

Kathy stood up. 'No chance. I'll go and get some chocolate and then you, Ms Hadley, are going to give me the delicious low-down on that Romeo of yours.'

It was a great party and the evening was even better. Kathy's grey stilettos made their second trip out in a week, but this time teamed with a dark violet dress, which again Alex had never seen, though Fleur assured him she'd had it for ages! Another trip to the hairdresser's did seem rather extravagant, though, and anyway by the time the tenpin party was over there wasn't any time. Instead, Fleur made do with a long, hot bath and her faithful old heated rollers.

Teetering along the street, holding a bottle in one hand

and Alex in the other, Fleur felt almost dizzy with expectation, the thrill of seeing Mario undiminished, even though it was by now an extremely regular event.

'This has been the best birthday, Mum.'

Fleur squeezed his hand. 'I'm glad, darling.'

'Maybe you should have a party, too,' Alex suggested hopefully. Fleur didn't answer straight away. Her last couple of birthdays hadn't been much fun, and she knew Alex felt it, too. Though she tried not to dwell, to wallow in her grief, her birthday was the one day she kept apart from the rest. It had been on her birthday that she and Rory had finally got engaged and put down the deposit on the house. Now it was the one day of the year that she kept just for Rory. Alex would make her a cup of tea and tunelessly sing 'Happy Birthday' and they might have a cake in the evening, but that was as far as it went, and that was how she liked it.

'Not this year, darling. Let's just keep my birthday between us Alex, OK?'

'Oh.'

Fleur stopped and turned. 'What's the matter?' Alex had a guilty look on his face that Fleur knew only too well. It was normally reserved for times when he'd said he'd done his homework or reader and Fleur asked to see it.

'I think I might have said something—to Mario, I mean. I was saying how your birthday was a couple of weeks after mine, how we normally didn't do much...'

'And what did Mario say?' Fleur sighed.

'Nothing really. Honest, Mum, he might not have even heard.'

Fat chance, Fleur thought. Well she'd have to have a word with Mario before, knowing him, he went ahead and booked a deluxe suite at the Windsor!

'Don't worry about it, Alex. You didn't do anything wrong.'

'You're not cross?'

Fleur laughed 'No, I'm not cross. Come on, we'd better get a move on, and these shoes are starting to hurt.'

Fleur had been wondering how on earth Teresa was going to fit the contents of the vast family tree of the Ruffinis under one roof, but as they made their way through the room, being kissed on both cheeks by everyone Mario enthusiastically introduced them to, Fleur saw the French windows led into a huge white marquee that had been set up for the occasion. And what an occasion! It looked more like a wedding than an engagement party. Rows and rows of tables laden with flowers were arranged around a huge dance floor, the band was already playing and several couples were happily dancing as children played chase and hide and seek under the starched white tablecloths.

'Fleur, so glad you could come.' Teresa kissed her in the customary fashion. 'I hope we're not too terrifying.'

'Not at all.' Fleur smiled. 'Everyone's being really friendly. Alex has already abandoned me.' She gestured to where Alex was playing happily with Ricky.

'I've put him on the children's table for dinner, I thought he might have more fun there.' Teresa looked over at the children rushing past. 'He's having a great time, isn't he?'

Alex *was* enjoying himself, Fleur thought as Mario took her arm and led her to the dance floor. In fact, over the last few weeks, since Mario had come into their lives, Alex had come on in leaps and bounds. The bed-wetting was history, he was making friends and he was far less uptight. As she relaxed against Mario, letting him guide her to the romantic beat of the music, she was aware of a couple of curious stares in her direction, most noticeably from one elderly woman who was openly scrutinising Fleur. Fleur flashed a tentative smile but when the woman looked distastefully away, Fleur merely shrugged. No doubt she had put a couple of noses out of joint by being here tonight but, instead of being anxious about upsetting anyone, for once in her life she couldn't have cared less. If anything, it gave her a frisson of delight. Let them look, let them be jealous, she thought. Mario's here with me.

'I hope you haven't eaten today.'

Fleur looked up. 'Not a thing, if you discount the chocolate Kathy forced on me. I took your advice, though I must admit I'm starving.'

'And you're glad you came?'

Nodding, she nestled back into his chest, swaying in time to the music and wishing the song would never end, but all too soon they were being guided to their tables, to be greeted with more kisses and 'pleased to meet yous'.

They started with melon and Parma ham and no sooner was that whisked away than a plate of whitebait was placed in front of her.

Mario laughed as he saw her face. 'It's delicious.'

'I'm sure it is, but you'd think they could have taken the heads off.'

Mario grinned. 'Try,' he said simply, tucking in.

Try she did, and Mario was right. They were delicious. The meal went on for ever, relaxed, unhurried, the endless courses broken up with dancing and socialising. A beautiful lasagne was next, packed with mozzarella cheese and prosciutto. Fleur tucked in unashamedly, even taking a second helping when the waiter passed by.

'That was the most delectable lasagne I've ever tasted,' she declared, putting down her knife and fork then dabbing her lips with her serviette. 'I hope there's a bit of break, though, before dessert. I'm full.'

This caused a ripple of laughter from Mario. 'We've got a long way to go before dessert. That was just the entrée.'

Fleur looked up with something akin to faint horror as the waiter removed her plate, only to be followed by another young man bearing breast of chicken wrapped around an olive and sun-dried tomato stuffing. Artichoke hearts and new potatoes were happily piled onto her plate as she took a large sip of water.

'I warned you,' Mario said, topping up their wine-glasses.

'You sat there and let me have two servings of lasagne, you beast,' she whispered. 'You're going to have to help me.'

'No way,' Mario said, attacking his chicken with his knife and fork. 'I want to save a bit of room for the Italian sausages.'

Luckily the Italian sausages didn't come around till later—much later. In between times Fleur had forced down the most delicious tiramisu she had ever tasted, as well as a couple of sambucas, and had danced and danced till her feet were numb. Watching Mario dive on the sausages as if he hadn't eaten for a week, Fleur settled for an extremely strong espresso.

'There you are.' Teresa came over holding two tired little boys with either hand. 'Ricky and Alex are completely exhausted. Mind you, I'm not surprised. They've been dancing for the last two hours.'

Fleur pulled Alex onto her knee. 'You've had a great time, haven't you? How about I find my bag and get you home?'

'But Teresa said I could stay,' Alex protested, wriggling down from Fleur's knee and looking pleadingly up to Teresa.

'I said that we'd ask your mum.' She smiled over to

Fleur. 'I can put up a campbed in Ricky's room. They're the best of friends all of a sudden.'

'But he stayed last week,' Fleur pointed out. 'I really don't want to impose.'

Teresa laughed easily. 'It's certainly not an imposition. Alex is a pleasure to have, compared with some of the monsters Ricky has befriended over the years. His manners are beautiful.'

'Well, as long as Ricky comes to us next week.'

To murmurs of 'Cool', the two boys scampered off with Teresa. Fleur turned to Mario. 'I can't believe I just did that. If you'd known the sleepless nights I had, worrying about the sleep-over last week, and now I'm agreeing to him staying here and he hasn't even got a toothbrush and pyjamas.'

Mario took her hands. 'See, it was easy after all. You know Teresa's great, you know he's going to be well looked after and now you've got Ricky coming next week. It's all good for Alex. Who knows? By next season you might even let him run out onto the footy field without that ridiculous contraption on his head.'

She was too mellow from the sambuca to get riled, so Mario pushed further.

'Maybe the following week Teresa might have Alex again. A little bird tells me you've got a birthday coming up.'

She wasn't that mellow! 'Mario, please, don't organise anything for my birthday. I honestly don't like a fuss.'

'Are you one of these women who never admit how old they are?' he teased.

Fleur let her fringe fall over her eyes. 'Something like that,' she muttered. It was better he thought that than know the truth and rush around trying to make things better. Some things just couldn't be fixed.

She was saved from further explanation as the band struck up a particularly romantic number and Mario practically dislocated her shoulder in his haste to get her onto the dance floor.

'Have you any idea how gorgeous you look in that dress?' His blue eyes were boring into her, glinting with passion and promise.

The sambuca was really kicking in now. Pulling him closer, she swayed against him, a wave of lust making her suddenly unsteady. Moving her lips to his ear, her words came out in a husky whisper. 'Have you any idea how much better I'd look with it off?'

It was all the incentive he needed, and they left the dance floor as abruptly as they'd joined it. Of course, because they were rushing, the goodbyes took ages. It seemed everyone in the room wanted to kiss them both, and when they finally made it into the warm night air they were giggling as they walked.

'They loved you,' he enthused. 'They all loved you.'

'Except for that lady in the blue dress,' Fleur pointed out. 'The one with the tight perm.'

'Ah, Zia Rafaella. Well, actually, she's not a real aunt but that's what we've always called her.'

'So why was she giving me dirty looks?'

'Well, you know I told you I'd have some dark-haired beauty to sit next to if you didn't come…'

Fleur looked up at him, her eyes wide. 'I thought you were joking.'

Mario laughed. 'Not at all, except in this case it's a bit more complicated.' The smile suddenly disappeared from his face. 'Fleur, there's something I need to tell you. How about you show me the beach where you do so much of your thinking?'

It was a short stroll to the beach where they took off

their shoes as they negotiated the rather steep descent. As they pulled back an old tea tree, the whole deserted beach lay before them. There was hardly a breath of wind, yet the inky black sea still rumbled loudly as it crashed into the cove, the waves breaking and sending ripples of surf onto the sandy beach. A full moon cast a luminous white glow, and hand in hand they walked through the surf.

'Zia Rafaella has a granddaughter, Carmella.'

'Was she the one lined up for you tonight?' Fleur cast her mind back. 'I don't remember being introduced.'

'No, you wouldn't have seen her. Carmella is in Italy.'

'Oh.'

They walked on for a while before he continued. 'As I said, Zia Rafaella is not a real aunt, she's a very dear family friend. More than an aunt really. Our families are very close.'

'And Carmella?' Fleur's voice was somewhat strangled but she managed to keep it even.

'My family arranged a date for me with her. Nothing new in that, of course, except this time it was a bit different.'

'In what way?'

'There was a second date.'

Fleur stopped walking, staring up at the huge moon. She knew what was coming next.

'And a third.'

'Do you love her?' It hurt to ask that, hurt more than Fleur could ever have imagined.

'No, but I do like her.'

'Don't tell me.' Fleur couldn't keep the bitterness from her voice. 'You *adore* her.'

Mario shook his head. 'Not even that. But, Fleur, she is a good woman, and had I carried on dating her I would have been expected to marry her. Much as I enjoyed her company, I didn't want that. But it would have been easy to carry on dating her. I enjoyed her company and we actually *did* get on. As I told you, my father is sick and he would love to see me married. There was just so much pressure from all corners for Carmella to be the one.'

'Have you slept with her?'

'No. I would never shame her like that. Had I slept with her I would have had to marry her. I know this is hard for you to understand, but it's just the way my family is.'

'But it's all right to sleep with me.'

'Fleur.' His voice was sharp. 'I am trying to explain how things are for me back home. I want to marry for love, I want to be sure that I've got it right. With my family, with Carmella, it's all or nothing and then there's no going back.'

'So that's why you came here?' Fleur was furious now. 'To prevent you from succumbing to your urges and sleeping with the gorgeous Carmella!'

'No! I came here because I didn't love her. Because I knew there was no point in it carrying on.'

His words reached her, calming the anger exploding inside her.

'I don't love Carmella,' he said emphatically, his words finally soothing her. 'I finished it before I came to Australia. Coming here made things look a bit more respectable for her. I had caused her enough pain, the last thing I wanted to do was shame her. I'm only telling you this because I believe in honesty. Fleur, can't you see how much you mean to me? If this were just a fling, then why would I jeopardise it by telling you about Carmella?'

'OK,' she grumbled, her face breaking into a smile. 'So you still adore only me?'

Mario took her hand and they started walking. 'Yes, Fleur, it's you alone that I adore.'

In silence now, they drifted along. Only when they collapsed against a sand dune, the scratchy pampas grass tickling her bare legs, did they speak again, and then it was the language of lovers entwined, secret whispers that carried in the night air drifting out over the vast ocean. He held her with such veneration, his body adoring her with each sweet kiss, each tender touch. And for the moment at least, Fleur truly believed that, despite the problems they faced, somehow, some way love would provide the answers.

CHAPTER TEN

'HAPPY birthday to you, happy birthday to you.'

Fleur sat up in bed, smiling brightly as Alex handed her the laden tray. Crunching her way through burnt toast and very milky tea, she read the card Alex had made her and opened her gift.

'Turkish delight, yum,' she lied, pulling him in beside her for a cuddle, 'And the card's just beautiful.'

'Perhaps we could go out tonight to the new pizza place?' Alex asked, ever hopeful.

'Maybe we'll do that at the weekend,' Fleur said, forcing her voice to remain bright. 'I'm on till four this afternoon so I'll be tired. Now, you'd better dive in the shower and get dressed. Ben will be here soon.'

Once she could hear the taps running Fleur tipped the tepid tea down the sink and made herself a good, strong, hot coffee. Choosing to read the paper in the kitchen, rather than face the living room and Rory's picture, she settled down at the kitchen table for now. Her thinking could wait until Ben and Alex were safely off at school.

Kathy arrived bang on time, as cheerful as ever. 'Look at you, still in your dressing-gown.'

'It is seven in the morning,' Fleur pointed out.

'And no doubt you've been lording it with breakfast in bed. Alex told me about his plans. Anyway, I'd better get off. I don't want Danny to punish me and stick me in the obs ward. I'm ready for some action today.'

'Well, just make sure the place is quiet by the time I get there,' Fleur joked. 'I could use a peaceful afternoon.'

As Kathy made her way down the path she turned casually. 'I promised Ben I'd take him to the new pizza place for tea. How about I bring Alex along? It will give you a bit of a breather after work. I can drop them off after we've all eaten, say around seven?'

'You're sure you don't mind? I'll shout the boys a burger at the weekend.'

'Deal,' Kathy said cheerfully, waving as she climbed into her car. 'By the way, happy birthday, Fleur!'

As Fleur walked Alex and Ben to their classrooms and said goodbye, all she wanted to do was go home and spend some time alone, but it just wasn't to be.

'Fleur?' Miss Donohoue, the boys' teacher, called her back as she made her way out of the classroom. 'I've just had a mum who was supposed to be helping in the gym this morning ring and cancel. It's a shame because the children were really looking forward to it, but I really need another adult to help. Is there any chance you could stay? It will only be for an hour.'

What could she say? The next hour was spent helping eight-year-olds clamber over various pieces of wooden apparatus, and by the time she got home, made the bed and cleared up the extraordinary mess Alex had left in the kitchen, there was barely enough time to jump in the shower and pull on her uniform. So much for a reflective morning, Fleur thought wryly as she drove off to work. Oh, well, at least Kathy had Alex this evening. She would go for a walk on the beach, and when Alex got home he could have an early night for once. She could do her thinking then.

There certainly wasn't any time for reflection at work. As usual the place was full to the rafters with patients waiting to be moved up to the wards and relatives growing increasingly impatient at the delays.

The relatives weren't the only tricky customers, she thought as she approached Mario for some assistance. 'Mr Gordon's IV has run through. I wondered if you could write up some further orders.' Fleur handed him the necessary paperwork as he sat 'on hold' on the telephone.

'He's a surgical patient,' Mario said crisply. 'I referred him three hours ago.'

'I know that,' Fleur answered patiently, somewhat surprised at his demeanour; Mario was usually more than helpful. 'He's been clerked in. Wendy just forgot to write up the IV orders. I've tried paging the surgical team a few times, but I can't get anyone down here.'

'Then send Mr Gordon to the ward. The doctor can write it up there.'

'There isn't a bed for him yet.' Exasperation was starting to creep into her voice. Fleur really didn't have time for this right now.

'No, I will not hold!' Cursing, he slammed down the telephone as Fleur stood there, stunned, with the IV sheet in her hand. 'Excuse me,' Mario quickly apologised. 'I have a fifty-year-old unconscious head injury, we have no ICU beds and I am attempting, though not very successfully, to arrange admission to another hospital. Unfortunately the bed manager there seems to think I have nothing better to do than sit and listen to piped music.'

Fleur gave a thin smile. 'Tell me about it. I have a boss who thinks I've nothing better to do than haggle over an IV order. Now, are you going to write it up or not?'

He took the sheet and wrote up the orders in his appalling handwriting, which would take an age to decipher, but in his present mood Fleur thought better than to mention it.

'Thank you,' she said curtly as he handed her the sheet.

'Fleur.'

'What?'

'Happy birthday.'

He looked as miserable as she felt, and this time when she smiled it was genuine. 'Why don't you try ringing the bed manager from the staffroom? At least you can drink coffee while you're put on hold.'

'I think I might just do that.'

That was the last she saw of him. The rest of the afternoon passed in a whirr of chasing beds, doctors and patients' files, and when the late staff returned from afternoon coffee Fleur was only too happy to hand over to the next shift and head for home.

Home. Fleur looked up from the beach where she was slowly meandering. She could see it so clearly from her viewpoint on the shore—the white weatherboard house, an array of flower-filled pots brightening the veranda, the tables and chairs where they took their meals. Nothing like the crumbling shed they'd purchased all those years ago. Even the real-estate agent had thought they were crazy when they'd put in their offer. It had been a run-down shack then, damp, with an outside toilet and no kitchen to speak of. But it had bay views, Rory had pointed out excitedly to their parents. And with a helluva lot of work it would be beautiful.

He'd been right. Every cent had been poured into the renovations. Weekends, when normal couples of their age had been out partying, had instead been spent at various hardware stores, or painting, sandpapering and plastering. Doing whatever needed to be done to make their tiny slice of Australia home. Ten years ago today they had put down the deposit and Rory had pulled a tiny box out of his jeans and asked her to be his wife. Tears pricked her eyes as she walked, more purposefully now. They'd had such big plans, so many dreams. They would work like crazy, pay off the mortgage in record time and then—who knew?—maybe private school for Alex, holidays on the Gold Coast. They'd had a whole lifetime glittering before them and they were going to make the very best of it.

She hadn't wanted to think about Mario today. It had seemed wrong somehow. But as she came to the sand dune where they'd made love, tears flowed unchecked down her cheeks. Would Rory understand? Would Rory approve? She truly didn't know. Twenty-somethings didn't talk about death, didn't discuss the possibility that they mightn't be around for ever. The chance that one day someone else might be raising the child they loved, holding the partner they cherished. If only she knew how he would have felt about it, maybe then she could move on.

'Fleur.' For a second she thought she was hearing things, but as she spun around and saw Mario there she hastily wiped her cheeks with the back of her hand.

'What are you doing here?'

'I tried the house. When there was no answer I thought that I might find you here. Seems I was right. I was hoping we could talk.'

'I was just walking, thinking…' She shrugged helplessly. As much as Fleur normally loved seeing him, she really needed to be alone tonight, with her thoughts, with her memories. If ever she and Mario were going to make it, she needed to make peace within herself first. 'It's really not a good time, Mario. Can it wait?'

'No, Fleur, what I have to say cannot wait.' His voice was serious and held no hint of negotiation. 'Let's walk.'

He held out his hand and Fleur hesitated a moment. Glancing down at her watch, she let out a groan. 'I've lost track of time. Alex will be back soon. We'd better go back to the house.'

But as Mario shook his head Fleur felt anger start to build in her. 'Don't worry, he's staying late at Kathy's.'

'What do you mean?'

'I spoke with Kathy. She said she would keep him until you rang—all night if needed. I have thought of everything.'

'No, you damn well haven't.' The anger in her voice surprised even Fleur. 'How dare you just go ahead and arrange a babysitter? I told you I didn't want any fuss about my birthday. But, oh, no, you just wouldn't listen, would you? You had to go right on ahead, ignoring my wishes and making plans. Didn't it ever occur to you that I meant what I said?'

He looked at her, perplexed. 'What on earth are you talking about, Fleur?'

'You know full well, Mario. You think you can swan in and fix everything with that smile of yours and a meal. Well, sometimes it takes a bit more than that, like listening and respecting another person's wishes.'

How she expected him to react to her outburst Fleur wasn't sure—an apology perhaps, some contrition at least. Never once did she anticipate the fury in his voice when he spoke.

'Well, how about *you* try listening to *me*? You don't have the monopoly on grief and problems, Fleur. It doesn't always have to be about you.'

'What's that supposed to mean?' she retorted furiously. 'I never asked you to come here. I never asked for all of this.'

'All of what?'

'This,' she said, gesturing wildly at the air around her. 'You think it's all so easy. That I can just drop everything and fall into your arms and it will all be all right. Well, there's a lot more to it than that. I have a son, a life. You can't just upend us both. How do I know you're not going to swan back to Rome in a few months, back to your precious Carmella? How do I know this isn't just a holiday romance, a final fling before you tie the knot?'

'A holiday romance?' The scorn in his voice was obvious. 'Is that what you think of me?'

It wasn't, of course it wasn't, but anger blurred her senses. 'How should I know?' Fleur retorted defensively, two angry spots of colour flaming on her pale cheeks. 'How do I know that a holiday romance isn't on your precious list of Melbourne's "must dos"?'

An elderly man, walking his dog, looked over curiously at the couple standing, arguing. 'We'll talk at the house,' Fleur said angrily, and with a toss of her head she marched off, only to be overtaken in an instant as he strode ahead of her.

Fuming, she tried to keep up with his long strides as Mario marched purposefully up the garden path. How dared he barge in on her private time and accuse her of being selfish? She hadn't asked him to come this evening. In fact, she'd specifically told him that she didn't want any fuss on her birthday. Why couldn't he have just left it at that?

They stood bristling with unvented anger in the hallway, the ringing of the telephone an unwelcome diversion.

'Leave it,' he snapped, but Fleur shook her head.

'Some of us have responsibilities.'

It was a cheap shot, and she knew it. Mario was probably the most responsible person she'd ever met. And though she didn't know quite where the row had blown in from, how they had got to be here, she certainly wasn't prepared to back down, not yet anyway.

But Mario, Rory, the row, everything all flew out of her

head as she heard Kathy's tearful voice on the other end of the telephone.

'Fleur, I've been trying to ring.'

'Where are you?' Fleur felt her stomach turn to liquid, icy fingers of fear clutching at her heart.

'At the hospital. There's been an accident. Alex is all right,' she continued quickly as Fleur sank into the chair beside the telephone. 'I mean, he's not seriously injured or anything. He fell off the trampoline. Fleur, I think he's broken his ankle. They're doing an X-ray now.'

Fleur didn't say anything, her hand clutching the telephone convulsively as Mario looked on anxiously.

'I didn't want to move him, so I called an ambulance. I could probably have taken him in the car but...' Her voice trailed off. 'I'm so sorry, Fleur.'

'I'm on my way,' Fleur said, running her tongue over her dry lips as she replaced the receiver. Trying to stand, her legs were shaking so violently she was forced to sit straight back down. 'Alex has had an accident,' she said in a flat, hollow voice.

Mario knelt before her, his blue eyes shocked, his voice full of concern. 'Is it serious?'

She found her feet then, jumping up violently. 'Of course it's bloody serious! He's broken his ankle. Kathy had to call an ambulance.' She was terrified, confused, spun into panic as she tried to find her handbag. 'And it's all your fault. Why couldn't you just leave it? Why did you have to go butting in, arranging birthday surprises with Kathy? He should have been at home with me!'

The trip to the hospital was a nightmare. Mario point blank refused to let her drive, given the state she was in, so her angry outburst continued unchecked until they screeched to a halt outside the hospital. Not once did he tell her to calm down or answer her furious accusations.

Only as she opened the car door did he pull her back for a second.

'Go easy on Kathy.'

Fleur didn't answer. She ran through the familiar department, steeling herself—for what, she didn't know.

'Fleur, he's in here.' Kathy had obviously been crying, her red eyes looking anxiously down the accident department's polished corridor as Fleur approached. 'I'm so sorry.'

Pulling back the curtain, Fleur blinked in surprise at the sight of Alex sitting up on a hospital trolley, a huge grin on his face. 'Hey, Mum, I'm going to get a plaster on my leg.'

Luke showed her the X-rays, a tiny greenstick fracture of the left malleolus, which would mean a plaster for six to eight weeks.

'Can I go to school tomorrow and show everyone?'

'Of course not,' Fleur answered quickly. 'You'll need to stay home for a few days at least.'

But Luke shook his head. 'Maybe not tomorrow, Alex. You ought really to keep your leg up so that your ankle doesn't swell, but I'm sure you'll be right to go back the next day.' He raised his eyes at Fleur. 'Boys, huh? They scare the life out of you, don't they? I'll see about getting a plaster put on.'

'I'm sorry, Fleur,' Kathy ventured again. 'I was watching him. They were just having a bounce on the trampoline and I was just about to call them in for the evening when he fell.'

'Well, if you hadn't concocted this charade with Mario, it never would have happened.' Even as she said it, Fleur knew she was wrong, knew she was being unfair. Mario, of course, walked in just as the words spilled out of her mouth. The look he gave her wasn't particularly pleasant, his face only softening when he saw Alex.

'Hey, sport, what have you been up to? Scaring your mum like that?'

'I'd better go.' Kathy was struggling not to start crying again. 'I'll ring tomorrow, Fleur, see how he is...' She hesitated in the doorway. 'I know we're both off duty tomorrow, but what about the next day? I mean, can I still look after him?'

Fleur should have reassured Kathy, she knew that. Should have said, Sure, it had been a simple accident, one that could have happened anywhere. But right here, right now, as she struggled with a range of emotions, Fleur simply wasn't up to putting others at ease.

'We'll talk tomorrow,' Fleur said shortly, ignoring the black look Mario threw at her.

It was a taxi or Mario's car, and Fleur seriously wished she had chosen the former when she glimpsed Mario's strained, taut profile as he drove the car to her home. But not once did his voice indicate that he and Fleur were having problems as he chatted amicably to Alex, though Fleur could tell from the white knuckles gripping the steering-wheel that he was far from happy.

'Why don't you try out the crutches tomorrow?' Mario suggested gently as he lifted Alex out of the car and carried him up the path. Fleur followed him as he carried Alex through the house and into his bedroom, helping Fleur as they struggled to get his school shorts over the plaster and the tired little boy into his pyjamas. 'Perhaps give him some paracetamol now,' he suggested, and when Fleur returned with the tablet and a glass of water she saw Alex, his leg raised on a couple of pillows, listening as Mario read him a bedtime story. Standing in the doorway, looking at them huddled on the bed she felt a sting of tears in her eyes.

'Here's your tablet, darling,' she said, making her way over. Alex, exhausted now, was asleep before Fleur had even flicked off the light.

'He's fine,' Mario said wearily when they reached the hallway. 'He'll be racing about tomorrow on his crutches.'

'I know,' Fleur admitted. 'I just got a fright.' Watching as he retrieved his car keys from his pocket, she suddenly didn't want him to go. She'd said so many terrible things, things that couldn't be left to simmer unchecked overnight. 'Stay,' she said urgently. 'At least for a coffee.'

But Mario shook his head. 'I really have to go.'

'But you wanted to talk.'

'It will keep for another time. You get some rest. It's been a big shock for you.'

He kissed her briefly, and though it wasn't on her cheek, for the depth of passion behind it, it might just as well have been.

From her lounge window she watched as his car weaved down the street, his indicator flashing as he turned onto the main beach road, and suddenly she was filled with a sense of dread. A terrible feeling that she'd left it too late and was never going to get the chance to say that she was sorry.

Rory's parents made Fleur's reaction the previous night look positively mild. Nothing Fleur said as they sobbed into the telephone could console them. They were old and frail and had lost their only child, so anything that happened to Alex truly terrified them.

'Honestly, Gina, he's fine. Look, why don't I bring him over?' Fleur suggested, rolling her eyes at the thought of a two-hour drive. 'Of course it's not a problem. Alex can put his leg up on the back seat for the journey, and then you can see for yourself that he's OK.'

Of course, once they were there they ended up staying for the day and Fleur had to field a barrage of questions with as much tact as she could muster.

'You shouldn't have gone back to work,' Gina said accusingly. 'It isn't right, having someone else to look after your children. It's not as if you need the money. Rory left you well provided for.'

'I know he did, but work's important to me, and Alex has really come on since I went back.'

'I wouldn't call a broken ankle coming on,' Gina said pointedly as she washed up after the evening meal. 'If he'd been home with his mother, none of this would have happened.'

The words were rather too familiar. 'Kathy's a wonderful friend,' Fleur said defensively. 'She looks after Alex as if he were her own child. It could have happened any time.' And as the words came out of her mouth the guilt that had been niggling suddenly multiplied dramatically. Imagine if it had happened to Ben while she'd been looking after him? Imagine having to ring Kathy and tell her, and worse, imagine how she would have felt if Kathy had then reacted the way she herself had? She had treated Kathy appallingly and the long drive home gave Fleur plenty of time to dwell on the fact.

Stopping to fill up with petrol, Fleur bought the biggest slab of chocolate the garage had in stock. Though it was late and Alex should really have been in bed, she pulled up outside Kathy's and knocked nervously on the door, unsure of her reception.

'I'm sorry,' Fleur blurted out as soon as the door opened. 'I treated you appallingly.'

Kathy stood there for a moment, her face unmoved. 'And you think a bar of chocolate can make up for it?'

Fleur didn't know what to say, but as Kathy's face broke into a huge grin she felt as if a huge weight had been lifted from her shoulders.

'Where's Alex?'

'In the car. He's fine, though I ought to get him home. I just wanted to let you know how sorry I am.'

'You must be sorry if you were going to give me this huge slab of chocolate and not even ask for a piece!'

Fleur managed a feeble grin. 'If that's what it takes.'

'Don't be daft.' Kathy laughed. 'I'll just let Greg know where I'm disappearing to. You go and start the car.'

'I really am sorry,' Fleur said again once Alex was tucked in bed and two huge mugs of hot chocolate were in their hands. 'I completely overreacted.'

'No, you didn't,' Kathy said kindly. 'Given the circumstances, I think you did pretty well. You've had enough bad luck to last you a lifetime. I felt terrible when it happened. It might sound strange and you might not believe me but I'd rather it had happened to Ben than Alex.'

Fleur nodded. 'I can understand that. It's so much harder when it's someone else's kid you're looking after.'

'And ringing you to say there'd been an accident was a nightmare. I knew you'd think the worst had happened, and I can't blame you, given what you've been through. Just when you'd started to let go a bit, loosen up, something like this goes and happens.' She broke the chocolate bar up and handed Fleur a huge piece. 'This isn't going to set you back years, is it? I mean, you're not going to go all strange again?'

'I'm actually thinking of installing twenty-four-hour video surveillance.' She grinned when she saw Kathy's expression. 'Just kidding. No, as Luke said, he's a boy and these sorts of things happen. I was actually more worried about him when he wasn't getting into scrapes. He's fine, I know that. It was just coming on top of yesterday. I don't know if I ever told you but my birthday's a sort of anniversary for Rory and I—that's why I try to keep it low key.'

'I had sort of guessed,' Kathy said gently. 'That was why I suggested taking the boys to the pizza place—to give you a bit of space.'

Fleur's chocolate, which she was dunking into her drink, dropped from her fingers. 'But I thought you'd arranged it with Mario?'

'Not at all. Mario came by about half an hour before Alex's accident. He'd been trying to get hold of you all afternoon. He was pretty upset, you know, about his dad and everything. I thought that by offering to have Alex for a while longer it would give you more of a chance to sort things out.'

The chocolate Fleur had just retrieved with a teaspoon dropped back in the cup with a clatter. 'Why was he upset about his dad?'

Kathy looked over, her face aghast. 'You mean he didn't tell you?'

Fleur shook her head. 'I never really gave him a chance to. Please, Kathy, what's going on?'

'His dad's very sick, Fleur,' Kathy said gently. 'He had a heart attack yesterday morning.' She stopped for a moment to let the news sink in before hitting her with the next bit. 'Mario's got to fly back to Italy. He wanted to see you, to tell you why he had to go back. He was worried how you'd take it.'

'Oh,' Fleur moaned, putting her head in her hands. 'I never even let him speak, just banged on about how difficult it was for me, how he was intruding on my grief, and all the time he was just trying to tell me his father was ill.

'I thought he was a bit off at work yesterday—I just assumed he was having a bad day. I never for a moment imagined there was such a reason behind it.' She looked up, tears filling her eyes as Kathy made her way over and put her arms around her. 'What have I done? He's never going to forgive me for this.'

'Of course he will, you big pudding. Everyone who knows you knows what you're like, but we all love you. "There goes Fleur, jumping in without looking!" We're all used to it now. Mario will understand. And anyway, he's not going for a couple of days yet so you can still say that you're sorry.'

Fleur looked over at the clock on the mantelpiece. 'Do you think I should try ringing him now?'

'I don't know,' Kathy said thoughtfully. 'I mean, it's after eleven. They might get a fright and think that it's the hospital in Italy ringing or something. I'm sure it can keep till morning. You're on an early, you'll be able to talk to him soon.' Giving her friend a big cuddle, Kathy suddenly laughed. 'One final thing, Fleur Hadley. If you ever try to tell me it's no big deal between you and Mario Ruffini, you're going to lose your chocolate buddy for life. Us married women need a bit of romance in our lives, even if it is someone else's!'

Fleur tried to smile, tried to be comforted by Kathy's reassurances, but the same sinking feeling she'd felt last night came back to haunt her. What if it wasn't all that simple, what if Mario didn't want to hear her excuses and couldn't forgive her selfishness?

What if, this time, she'd really blown it?

CHAPTER ELEVEN

'YOU, my darling, really are a sight for sore eyes.' Delorus's beaming grin greeted Fleur as she walked into the department next day.

'I know you're lying, Delorus. I never slept a wink last night. I must look a real mess.'

'I don't care how you look, honey. Just the sight of you means that I'm going home soon, though I don't know why I'm bothering—I have to be back here at ten.'

Fleur nodded. 'I know. Danny said that you had a hospital appointment this morning, so if you want to hand over Resus to me and get off home a bit early, that's fine.'

'Are you sure? You're not supposed to start for another twenty minutes.'

'Honestly, Delorus, it's not often I'm early, what with Alex and everything, so why not make the most of it?'

'There's only the one in there at the moment, a Frank Hadley. No relation of yours, he assures me,' Delorus added anxiously. 'Anyway, he came in with chest pain around five a.m. His ECG was inconclusive and we're awaiting his blood results. Cardiology has seen him and think that he's probably got angina rather than having a heart attack. He looks too well to be in Resus really but, given the history I think we ought to keep him on a monitor. Once we've got the bloods back they're going to decide where to admit him. Frank insists he's going home once nine o'clock comes and his pension card gets him onto the bus. He's a cantankerous old man but a honey really.'

Delorus loved nothing more than a chat, and would have carried on happily if Fleur didn't speed things along. 'Has he had anything for pain?' Fleur asked, looking at his admission sheet.

'Just two GTN and we've put on a patch. He was hypertensive on admission but his blood pressure's coming down nicely now. There's no relatives with him, just a brother who lives in New South Wales who must be as old as him so I thought it might be better to wait for the morning before scaring the old boy. Who knows what could happen?'

'Fine. All right, Delorus, off you go.'

Delorus picked up her bag. 'One other thing, Fleur. I know it's more a ward problem, but I've been having a chat with Frank, you know, like I do…'

Fleur grinned. 'I know only too well.'

'He's a lonely old boy, a bit down on his luck at the moment. I think there's a lot of financial problems there, so could you just mention it to the ward staff? Maybe a social worker referral wouldn't go amiss.'

Fleur nodded. 'I'll pass it on.'

'He also reckons he's a friend of Mario's, wants to see him when he comes on. I said to him, "Honey, don't we all—?"'

'Delorus!' Fleur pointed to her watch. *'Go!'*

If Delorus was a good talker, Frank Hadley was an expert—a real tough old Aussie battler who, despite the oxygen mask, chattered away in his deep, booming voice.

'Hopefully your blood results shouldn't be too much longer, but I'll order you a breakfast from the kitchen just in case,' Fleur offered.

'Yeah, and charge me a fortune. I'll ring me neighbour later, she'll make me up some sandwiches and a Thermos of tea. That's if I decide to stay,' he added.

'It's free, Frank, we don't charge for meals here.'

'Huh,' he puffed. 'I'll believe that when I see it.'

'Honestly, Frank,' Fleur assured him. 'This is a public hospital, you're not going to get a bill for anything. Now, how about that breakfast?'

'No, thanks, I'll wait till I've spoken to me mate Mario, he'll give it to me straight. Did you know I was a good friend of your boss? Him and me go bowling together.'

Fleur suppressed a smile, thinking what an extraordinary pair they must make. 'He did mention something about it,' she admitted. 'Will you at least let me get you a cup of tea? I don't want Mr Ruffini thinking I haven't been taking good care of you.'

That seemed to work and grudgingly Frank accepted her offer. 'And I suppose I could force down a couple of slices of toast and Vegemite,' he added, as if doing Fleur a favour.

As Fleur set about checking the equipment in Resus, Frank tucked into his breakfast. 'So what time does me mate get in, then?'

'Normally around eight-thirty,' Fleur answered, without looking up from the oxygen cylinder she was checking.

'Works hard, doesn't he?' Frank nattered on, slurping his tea. 'Good bloke, though, and that's saying something. I'm not normally taken with foreigners.'

'You're not going to start talking about the war?' Fleur asked good-naturedly, and Frank actually laughed.

'He's helped me a lot. It's been a bit lonely for me since me wife died, not that you'd understand, of course. I've had a few problems and Mario, well, he sort of helps without you realising. You know, the odd game of bowling, a beer or two. He loves a yarn does Mario.

'I was a bit strapped for cash the other week. I never told him, though. And do you know, the same day that

I'm worrying about the rent he asks if he can buy my tenpin bowling shoes from me. My Elsie got them for me one Christmas—she thought that lawn and tenpin bowling were the same thing, God rest her soul. Mario didn't know that I was broke, mind, a bloke's got some pride. But I tell you this much, if he hadn't been around that day I don't know how I'd have found the rent. It was giving me a real headache.'

Fleur thought of how she and Kathy had howled with laughter at Mario's bowling shoes. She didn't feel guilty, it had just been a joke, but... She looked across the room at the difficult man lying on the trolley. A tough old guy, suspicious of the world and lonely as hell, yet Mario in his own very unique way had taken the time to help.

Walking over, Fleur took the empty plate and cup off his lap and replaced his oxygen mask. 'At your time of life, Frank, you shouldn't have to be worrying where the rent's coming from. Why don't I organise someone to come and have a chat with you once you're feeling a bit better?'

'One of those blooming social workers, sticking their noses in and telling me what to do?'

'Nobody's going to tell you what to do, Frank, but maybe someone "sticking their nose in" as you call it, might see things a bit differently and make sure you're getting all the benefits you deserve. Why not give it a try?'

Frank started to cry—not a lot, but enough that Fleur handed him a wad of tissues from the box on the window-ledge, keeping a couple for herself.

'It's just so hard and it keeps getting harder. I miss my Elsie so much. She always took care of the bills and house-keeping, everything really. I just wonder when the pain's going to go...'

Fleur took his rough, wrinkled hand in hers and held it

for a moment, blowing her nose with the other. 'I know, Frank,' she said gently. 'I know.'

'Fleur, sorry to interrupt.' Felicity popped her head around the sliding door. 'Mr Richardson wants to see you and Danny in his office. I can take over in here.'

Fleur squeezed the old man's hand. 'Hopefully I shan't be long.'

Walking into Luke's office, she half expected a query about a patient's treatment, a budget concern or perhaps, as was often the case unfortunately in Accident and Emergency, a complaint to be answered. Any of these she could have dealt with, anything other than the news that greeted her.

'I'll try not to hold you up.' Luke closed the door behind them. 'But I had some rather upsetting news last night from Mario. I thought I should tell you first and you can fill in the junior staff.'

Fleur stood straight, her face impassive, belying the violent dive her stomach had just taken.

'Apparently his father suffered a cardiac arrest yesterday afternoon. It seemed he survived the event but, as you can imagine, he's not a well man. Mario flew directly home which, unfortunately for us, leaves us down a man, a good man at that.'

'He'll be coming back, though?' Danny asked, echoing Fleur's immediate thought, but Luke shrugged noncomittally.

'Hard to say. For now he's taken annual leave, but I guess it all really depends on how his father does or doesn't do. Italy's hardly a destination he can pop back to at weekends. We're just going to have to play it by ear for now.'

The hospital wasn't the place to cry, to break down. No one there knew what Mario meant to her, and that had been her choice, she recalled. So the brutal news, delivered without padding or sentiment, had to be taken in a professional way.

'Thanks for letting us know, Luke.' She turned to go then hesitated, her mind working ten to the dozen. 'Perhaps we should send some flowers or something? If you've got an address, I'd be happy to organise it.' At least if she had an address she could contact him, tell Mario how sorry she was, not just for her behaviour but for what he must be going through.

But her attempt to put things right yet again proved fruitless. 'Good idea, Fleur, but I think we'd better wait a couple of days to make sure we're putting the right message on the card.'

Fleur gave a brief nod. 'You're right. Oh, well, I'd better get back to it.'

'Sister Hadley here tells me you're a good friend of Mr Ruffini's.' Dr Lupen peered over his glasses at Frank.

'He's me bowling partner,' Frank said proudly.

'Well, I'm sure he'd have liked to have seen you for himself, but as that's not possible I'd better make sure you're well looked after. We'll get you moved directly up to the ward, Mr Hadley, and thank you for being so patient. I know it's been a long wait.'

After settling Frank into bed on the coronary care unit, Fleur went over to the nurses' station and gave her handover to the charge nurse, relaying the tests and investigations that had been carried out in the emergency department.

'Dr Lupen says we're to give Mr Hadley the five-star treatment.'

Fleur laughed. 'Actually, it was very good of him to play along with it. Mr Hadley was pretty cantankerous when he came in, though you wouldn't think it, looking at him. He's like a teddy bear now.'

She relayed the story of how Mario had befriended him and how it had brought the barriers down. 'So any time he refuses his meds or threatens to go home, just tell him Mario would be horrified if he thought you weren't treating him properly, how it's more than your job's worth—that sort of thing. It works a treat.'

The charge nurse grinned. 'Don't worry, we'll give him five-star treatment. Poor old boy, it must be hard, being on your own. He sounds nice, that Mr Ruffini. We could do with a few more like him around the place.'

Couldn't we just? Fleur thought as she wandered slowly back to the ward. But how many Mario Ruffinis were there in the world? He was a one-off, unique. Yet again he'd taken a horrible situation and made it just that bit better. Not just for the likes of Mr Hadley and Mrs Levitski, but for all the staff.

Everything he'd touched he'd turned around, from the comradeship and team spirit right down to the coffee they all drank. He had changed things for her and Alex, too. Slowly, so slowly he'd shown them the way back to the outside world, shown them how sweet and good life could be, if only you let it.

And what had she done for him? Screamed at him on the beach when he'd tried to tell her about his father, shown him the worst possible side of her nature the one and only time he'd really needed her.

'What are you doing, dawdling? You know that Danny will be screaming for you!'

'Delorus.' Fleur jumped as the familiar voice broke into her thoughts. 'How was your appointment?'

'Fine. But can I go home? Oh, no, I come out of the doctor's room and the receptionist tells me Danny wants me to drop in on my way home, as if I don't spend half my life here already! Anyway, you take your time, honey. I'd best dash if I want any sleep today.' And without waiting for a response she bustled off down the corridor, muttering furiously to herself.

For once Fleur *did* take her time. Danny could wait. She couldn't believe there was no chance of bumping into Mario, no chance he would suddenly appear at the coffee-machine or yell at her in Resus. No chance he would knock on her door tonight and suggest he and Alex cook dinner on the barbie. Mario was gone now, back to his family, back to Italy, back where he belonged. And, though it terrified her even to think it, back to Carmella.

And she hadn't even said goodbye.

'There you are,' Felicity greeted her as she returned to the department. 'We were just about to send out a search party.'

'Why, is there someone new in Resus?'

'No, deadly quiet.'

Fleur raised a feeble grin. 'You've jinxed me now.'

'Danny wants you in his office.'

Fleur rolled her eyes. 'What have I done this time?'

'Don't ask me, but he said that you were to go straight there and I was to take over Resus.'

The last thing Fleur needed was a morning going over staff rosters and budgets. At least out on the floor she could immerse herself in her patients' problems—anything beat her own at the moment. Opening the office door, the first thing that hit her was the most delicious smell. Sitting on the desk was a vast red box containing pizza. Rather more surprising were the faces of Delorus and Kathy, with Danny sitting between them.

'What's going on?' Fleur asked suspiciously.

'That's what we were hoping to find out,' Danny said,

pushing the box in her direction. 'And as pizza worked so well in the staff meeting, I thought we might give it a try here.'

'What are you talking about?' Fleur asked, bemused.

'Honey.' Delorus folded her arms across her enormous bosom and fixed her with a steely glare. 'I have been up for twenty hours now and I want my bed, so why don't you sit down tell us what's going on with you and Mario so's we can work out what you're going to do? Then I might just get some shut-eye.'

'Kathy,' Fleur wailed. 'You promised you wouldn't say a word.'

'She didn't, well, not until this morning when I rang her. We all knew, Fleur. It stood out a mile off. Mario Ruffini is positively smitten with you. And if there was any room for doubt, you and him arriving together when Alex had his accident only confirmed things. So let's stop wasting time and get down to it.'

With a suspicious look Fleur rather reluctantly sat down. 'It won't do any good,' she warned. 'You know as well as I do he's in Rome.'

'Tell us anyway,' Delorus said as she deftly divided up the pizza.

They might as well have shone their pocket torches in her eyes. Stumbling at first, but gaining in momentum as she went along, Fleur told them her story, not all of it, of course—there were some bits too precious for sharing. And her three friends and colleagues listened as she spoke. Not commenting at all, just munching on their pizza as Fleur recounted the sorry tale.

'So,' Delorus asked as Fleur's story concluded, 'if he were here now, what would you say to him?'

'This isn't a set-up, is it?' Fleur said nervously. 'He's not hiding in the cupboard or anything.'

'You wish! No, honey, he's not here, so come on—what would you say to him?'

'That I'm sorry, I guess.'

'Sorry for what?'

'For not giving him a chance to speak, for being so wrapped in myself—'

'For not being there when he needed you?' Danny suggested.

'Something like that,' Fleur admitted reluctantly. 'I know I've been wrong. I was all set to say sorry when all this went and happened, but there's nothing I can do about it now. At least, not until I can get hold of a telephone number. Perhaps I should ring the hospital in Rome, ask to speak with him—'

'Since when did you start speaking Italian?' Kathy pointed out. 'You'd never get past the switchboard. Anyway, there are some things that can't be said over the telephone.'

'And some things that can't wait,' Delorus added.

'Great,' Fleur sighed. 'I told you there was nothing that could be done, unless I jump on plane and fly off to Italy myself. It looks like I've made a real mess of things...' She sat there waiting for a response, a clue as to what she should do now, but her friends just stared back at her, not saying word, their eyes holding hers as the silence grew ever louder. 'You surely don't think...' Fleur's eyes widened '...that I should fly to Italy, for heaven's sake? That's the most ridiculous suggestion I've ever heard.'

'Is it?' Danny said bluntly. 'You mean more ridiculous than sitting here doing nothing, giving up without a fight?'

'I've got an eight-year-old son with a broken ankle. I can hardly just hop on a plane. Alex has to come first.'

'Fleur, nobody's disputing that,' Kathy said gently. 'Of course Alex is your priority, he always will be. But if you've any hope of having a relationship with anyone, and I'm not just talking specifically about you and Mario here, there have to be times when your partner's needs take precedence. Everyone needs to come first sometimes. It doesn't mean you love Alex any less, it simply means that you might have to spread yourself a bit thin for a while. Mario needs you now. If you wait till his father's better or, heaven forbid, dead, sorry might not be enough. If you're not going to be there for him when he needs you the most, there's really not much point.'

'She's right,' Danny said sadly. 'I let Geoff down with his mother. It's only the fact we've been together so long that we survived it. You haven't got that luxury with Mario. You've got a passport?' he added as Fleur sat there stunned.

'And a credit card?' Delorus said, coming around the desk and wrapping her arms around her.

Kathy came, too. Crouching down, she took her friend's trembling hands in hers. 'And you've got a babysitter who's going to wrap your little treasure in a wad of cotton wool and never let him out of her sight. Anyway, he's not going to be able to get up to much mischief with that plaster on his leg.'

'I wouldn't bet on it,' Fleur sniffed. 'It's too much to ask, Kathy. You've got work, Ben, Greg.'

'Danny and I will work out the roster. There's two new staff starting tomorrow anyway. And don't think you're getting off scot-free. I've decided I need a bit more romance in my life, too, so Greg and I might just head off to Bali in a few months' time. You can return the favour then.'

'I mightn't get a flight,' Fleur said in a last futile attempt to halt the proceedings, but Delorus just laughed.

'Honey, there's a flight at seven tonight with your name

on it—you didn't think we'd leave out a detail like that, did you? You've just got to pay for your ticket at the check-in desk. Now, if all that's sorted I'm off to bed.' Her knees creaked as she stood up. 'You be sure to give that gorgeous Mario a big kiss from Delorus—don't you dare forget. You're not scared of flying, are you?'

Fleur shook her head 'No, at least I don't think so. I've actually never flown before.'

Delorus flashed her gorgeous grin. 'Well, honey, there's one way to find out.'

Alex took the news amazingly well and Fleur couldn't help but marvel in the change from the nervous, shy boy of just a few months before. Sitting on the veranda, a milk moustache on his freckled face, he fixed his direct gaze on Fleur. 'Is his dad going to die?'

'I don't know, Alex,' she answered honestly. 'It sounds as if he's very sick.'

'And Mario's with his dad now?'

'He's on his way to him,' Fleur said gently, her eyes filling with tears as she thought of Mario so proud and strong, sitting alone on the plane, his heart filled with despair at his inability in this instance to do a single thing.

'Will he come back? I mean, are you going to bring him back with you? I'm going to really miss him otherwise.'

Fleur looked out at the ocean, desperately trying not to break down, her voice trembling with emotion. 'I wish I could say yes, I wish I could give you that, but again, Alex, I just don't know. All I do know is that Mario had been good to us, *very* good to us. Even if he can't come back to Australia, I think he deserves a proper thank you, don't you?' She turned her troubled eyes to him, her heart bursting with love as she looked at his pensive little face.

'Maybe I could give you a card to take from me. I could

draw him a picture of the Tigers,' he suggested. 'He must be feeling really sad at the moment. It might cheer him up.'

'I think that's a wonderful idea,' Fleur said as he walked over to join her, their eyes looking up into the clear blue sky, focussing on the tiny silver glint of an aeroplane carrying its passengers to their destination. 'I won't be gone long, sweetheart, and I'll ring every day. You do understand, don't you?'

Alex nodded, his face breaking in a wide grin. 'Will I get a present?'

Fleur ruffled his hair. 'Oh, I would think so. Maybe while I'm away you can have a big think about what you'd like me to bring you back and then you can tell me on the telephone. Come on, darling, we'd better get packed. I'm supposed to be at Kathy's in an hour.'

Saying goodbye to Alex was agony, and only made worse as Fleur wasn't sure she was doing the right thing. Her instinct was to stay with her son. What on earth was she thinking, heading to the other side of the world? Yet part of her knew that for once in her life she had to follow her heart, no matter how difficult the journey. Fleur and Kathy had decided against taking Alex to the airport, realising it might be a bit much for all concerned. That trip could wait for Fleur's return. Pulling his little sturdy body into her arms, she bit hard on her lip to stop herself crying, smelling the apple scent of his shampoo, the mint of his toothpaste.

'I'm not going to tell you to be good, sweetheart, because I know you will be. I'm just going to tell you that Mummy loves you very much and she'll be home soon. Here.' She handed him one of Rory's wallets and Alex opened it, wide-eyed.

'Is that all for me?'

Fleur nodded. 'But be sensible. Maybe you can take everyone out for tea at the pizza place or burger bar a couple of times.' She gave him another kiss before turning quickly so he wouldn't see her tears.

'You'd better go if you want to get that plane,' Greg said gruffly, giving her a hug as Kathy hooted in the driveway.

Waving, smiling, she held it together until the car rounded the corner and she could finally break down. Kathy didn't say anything, just handed her a tissue from the dashboard as she battled the peak-hour traffic. Only when they had made it through the city and were heading down Flemington Road, the signs for the airport becoming more frequent, did Fleur finally manage to stop the tears.

'Feel a bit better?'

'Not really. He'll be all right, won't he? I don't mean with you looking after him or anything like that, I mean with me leaving him at such short notice.'

'Fleur, a couple of months ago I couldn't have even imagined this moment, but Alex is a different boy now. He's happy and he's confident and he knows his mum will be home soon. Hell, businesswomen do it all the time. Stop beating yourself up. There's a slab of chocolate in the glove-box,' she added. 'Break me off some.'

'I'll bring you back loads.'

Kathy laughed. 'You'd never get it through customs. I'll just have to settle for some gorgeous Italian shoes—you know my size.'

'Cripes,' Fleur gulped. 'I still haven't given you back the grey ones.'

'And no doubt you just happened to pack them "by accident"?'

'Well, I was rushing,' Fleur said guiltily. 'At this rate I'm going to need an extra case just for all the presents I'll have to bring back!'

'Guilt,' Kathy said dryly. 'Don't you just love it?'

CHAPTER TWELVE

THE first leg of the journey was horrendous. Fleur sat seemingly surrounded by happy families and couples, all safe and content in their two by two world.

As the captain gave the time at their destinations she realised it was morning in Italy. Mario would be landing now or on his way to his father, maybe already at his side. And though it hurt like hell to leave Alex, deep down Fleur finally knew she was doing the right thing. She gave up on the eye mask an attendant had handed out when it grew soggy from her tears and instead put on some headphones, staring unseeing at a film before finally drifting off into an unsettled sleep.

She rang Alex from Singapore, which entailed Kathy dragging him out of the shower so he could say hi to his mum. Thankfully there were no tears or worries. If anything, he was having a ball.

'I love you, Mum.'

'I love you, too, Alex.'

The hour or so in transit was spent exchanging money, spraying perfume and trying on lipsticks, as well as compulsively checking and rechecking her bag for her tickets and passport.

Clipping on her seat belt for the long-haul flight, finally Fleur felt better. As the jet lifted into the air, the lights of Singapore disappearing as they soared through the sky, Fleur found the hum of the aircraft comforting. Trapped in her own time capsule, here the world was on hold, and for now at least there was absolutely nothing she could do. It was strangely relaxing.

Accepting a glass of wine with her meal, she put on her headphones and fiddled with the controls, the beautiful fluid voice of Bocelli surrounding her. Suddenly she was lying in her bath, with candles flickering. She recalled the joy she'd felt then, that night when Mario had brought Ricky to do his homework. The tiny seed of love that had been planted, those first shy kisses, a growing sexual awareness. Who would have thought then that it would have come to this? That she, Fleur, would be embarking on an impulsive journey to the other side of the world, with no accommodation organised, no idea where she was going except for a piece of paper with the name of a hospital and an address that Danny 'thought' must be that of Mario's parents. It was the most crazy, spontaneous, scary thing she had ever done in her life, yet there was no place she would rather be right now.

Breakfast had been served, eaten and cleared away. The film had long since ended and now the screen in front of her was filled with a map. She watched the image of their plane transposed on the map, inching its way nearer Rome, every minute a fraction closer to Mario. As the captain announced their descent, the seat-belt sign lit up and the cabin lights dimmed, Fleur sat quite still, her eyes focussed on the screen. 'I'm coming, Mario,' she whispered quietly. 'I'm coming.'

Fleur's vision of dashing off the plane into a taxi was soon disillusioned. Handing over her passport and ticket at passport control, she waited what seemed an interminably long time as the impassive face of the official tapped away on his computer.

'English?'

'No, Australian,' Fleur said nervously.

'I mean you speak only English?'

Fleur swallowed nervously. 'Yes.'

'And you book this ticket only yesterday?' His accent was thicker and heavier than Mario's, and Fleur had to strain to understand.

'That's right. I have a friend, you see. His father is very sick.'

'And where you stay?'

Fleur chewed nervously on her lip. She remembered reading somewhere to look these people directly in the eye to show that you were telling the truth. 'I don't know yet, it was all rather rushed. I'm going to find a hotel once I've been to the hospital. Here...' she handed him the piece of paper with the hospital name on it, which he barely even gave a cursory glance.

'Is this *friend* meeting you?'

The suspicion in his voice was too much and Fleur's eyes filled with tears. Surely she couldn't have come this far to be defeated at the final hurdle?

'He doesn't know that I'm coming,' Fleur faltered, trying to compose herself, trying to look him in the eye. It was imperative that he believe her. 'We had a row, and then his father was taken ill. I just need to get to the hospital, to make sure he's all right. Please,' she added desperately.

Watching, her lungs bursting with the breath she was holding, she saw his hand pick up the rubber stamp and with a loud click the official stamped her passport.

'I 'ope things go well for you.'

For a second she was tempted to kiss him—wasn't that what all the Italians did? Instead, Fleur gratefully accepted her passport. 'Thank you,' she said simply, before making her way to the baggage area.

Round and round the baggage carousel went as she jostled for a space amongst the exuberantly vocal locals. And just when she was sure her luggage must surely be lost and she would have to venture over to *Informazione*, her suitcase appeared, small and dog-eared compared to the rest, but never had she been so delighted to see it. It was so light that Fleur didn't even bother with a trolley as she walked through Customs, half expecting to be stopped, half expecting yet another obstacle to be thrown in her path.

But suddenly she was through, stepping into a throng of people, couples, children and families all reuniting. Such was her longing she half expected Mario to appear from the crowd, to fight his way over and take her in his arms.

Never had she felt more alone.

The taxi rank was just as busy, but at least it moved quickly. Coming from the hot spring weather in Melbourne, Fleur thought she'd never felt so cold, her thin jacket offering little protection against the cold wind that was biting at her.

As Fleur stepped into a taxi, her nerves really hit home. What if the driver didn't understand her? What if he took her somewhere else, or they had an accident?

She handed him the piece of paper and he looked at the hospital's name before turning to face her.

'English?'

'Australian.'

The taxi driver grinned. 'Ah, Olympics!'

Rome was beautiful, breathtakingly so. That twenty-minute taxi ride, as they hurtled through the city on the 'wrong' side of the road, would have been savoured if she wasn't so nervous of meeting Mario. With horn blaring, they dodged scooters and pedestrians. Fleur gazed in awe at the seemingly endless numbers of beautiful men and women rushing to work dressed in long dark raincoats with bright scarves trailing, all so effortlessly elegant.

The taxi driver pointed out some of the more familiar landmarks, and Fleur gazed in wonder as they passed the Colosseum, truly unable to believe that she was really there and vowing that she would come back one day with Alex and Mario, only to chide herself for her brazen presumption.

As they drew up at the hospital Fleur fumbled in her purse, trying to work out the alien money.

''Ere.' The taxi driver took a note and showed her the fare, extracting some change from a small machine on his dashboard.

'*Grazie,*' Fleur said, refusing the change as she utilised practically the entire range of her Italian vocabulary.

The hospital was huge, a massive old building with a grand staircase leading to the entrance, a stark contrast to the modern Australian hospitals she was used to. But once inside it was every bit as high-tech as home, probably more so, Fleur mused. She stood in the huge foyer trying to read the multitude of signs before giving up and heading to the desk.

A young, immaculately made-up woman smiled at her curiously. It was only then that Fleur realised what a sight she must look in her thin clothes, with messy unkempt hair.

'*Posso aiutare?*'

'Mario Ruffini,' Fleur said slowly. 'I believe his father, Dr Ruffini, is a patient here.'

The woman shook her head at Fleur's attempt.

'Dr Ruffini,' Fleur said imploringly, and pointed to her chest, patting her hand on her heart. 'He is sick.'

'*Un momento, signora.*' The woman's beautifully manicured fingers tapped away at her keyboard.

'*Si, si. Dottore Ruffini, è un patienté al terzo piano.*' She looked at Fleur's noncomprehending expression. '*Aspetta ti porto.*'

Fleur shook her head, watching helplessly as the woman spoke rapidly in Italian to another girl on the desk, before making her way around.

'Come.'

'Thank you. I mean, *grazie.*' Fleur's linguistic skills were truly amazing!

The young woman walked incredibly quickly along the beautifully tiled corridors and Fleur struggled to keep up with her as she battled with her suitcase. In the lift she was painfully aware of the young woman's undisguised scrutiny. Fleur so badly wanted to dive into the toilets to at least run a comb through her hair and put on some make-up, to at least offer some competition to the undoubtedly stunning Carmella, but she could hardly explain that! Still, Fleur consoled herself, she was finally going to see Mario. Somehow she had made them understand her! Surely make-up wasn't important at a time like this?

Maybe not, but every little helps, Fleur thought as the ward doors swung open and again she was the recipient of a few raised eyebrows. Bracing herself for the sight of Mario, she felt her confidence plummet as she realised the ward was empty of visitors.

Her escort spoke rapidly to a nurse who with a smile beckoned for her to follow, leading her to a small side ward.

As she entered, for a second Fleur stood stunned. The face that lay with its eyes closed on the pillow was Mario's, just slightly more lined, the hair fanning grey at the sides. He was so pale and so very still, and only the slight movement in his chest and the steady bleeping of the heart monitor indicated that Dr Ruffini was alive.

Fleur turned to the nurse. How on earth was she going to explain this?

'Er, Dr Ruffini, he has a son.' Fleur sighed, impatient with herself at her inability to communicate. '*Bambino*,' she said hopefully, knowing deep down that it was useless. 'Dr Ruffini.' Fleur pointed to the bed. 'His *bambino*.'

The nurse was giving her really strange looks now as Fleur practically danced on the spot in her efforts to explain.

'Am I right in thinking that you're referring to my son?'

Fleur practically jumped out of her skin as Dr Ruffini suddenly spoke, his voice positively dripping with an upper-crust English accent.

'You speak English!' Never had she been so pleased to hear her own language.

'Extremely well.' Dr Ruffini smiled and Fleur saw the sapphire blue eyes that were so familiar. 'You must be Fleur.'

'But how do you know?' she gasped.

'Oh, just a logical assumption. My son has spent the last couple of months going on about a rather special Australian blonde. I think you fit the bill quite nicely.'

'I need to speak to him,' Fleur said imploringly, her voice filled with relief and desperation.

Dr Ruffini spoke to the nurse before translating back to Fleur. 'My son needs to speak with you, also. Apparently Mario is taking a moment while I rest to try and locate you. He is in Sister's office, attempting to ring you, at this very moment. Somehow I don't fancy his chances, do you? The nurse here will take you now.'

As she made to go, Fleur swung around, horrified. 'How rude of me. I didn't even ask how you were.'

Dr Ruffini lay back on his pillow, a smile creeping across his tired face. 'Lucky to be alive,' he said slowly.

'And very glad, too, I might add. I wouldn't have missed this for the world.'

As the nurse led her down the ward and motioned to a door, Fleur's hand paused before she knocked and instead she tentatively pushed down the handle. Quietly stepping inside, she was greeted with the delicious sight of Mario's wide back, his hands gesturing angrily as he spoke loudly into the telephone.

'What on earth do you mean, things will seem better soon, Delorus? It is imperative that I have her telephone number this instant.' He sighed loudly. 'I don't give a damn about hospital policy—'

'Mario.' She watched as his shoulders stiffened and agonisingly slowly his head turned, an incredulous look on his face.

'Fleur,' he gasped, dropping the telephone as he rushed across the room. 'Fleur, is it really you?'

Taking her in his arms, he kissed her frozen face, his lips warming hers as she fell into his arms, holding her close, his tears mingling with her own. It was only when they pulled apart, when she gazed breathless and speechless into his eyes, that they realised the telephone was still off the hook. Still holding her with one hand, he retrieved the receiver.

'Yes, Delorus, you were right. Things do seem one helluva lot better all of a sudden.' He listened for a moment, smiling as he did so. 'I'll be sure to tell her.'

'What did she say?' Fleur asked, trembling as she stood there.

'That you promised to give me a kiss from her, and I will hold you to that, too. But first, Fleur, tell me, why *are* you here?'

'Isn't it obvious?' She stared back at him, trembling violently now as the moment of truth dawned. 'It's because

I love you, Mario, that's why I'm here. And because I'm so sorry for letting you down.' The tears were rolling down her cheeks and Mario sat down, pulling her onto his knee as he did so.

'But, Fleur, you never, ever let me down. What on earth gave you that idea?'

'On the beach,' she sobbed. 'You were trying to tell me that your father was sick and I didn't even give you a chance. All I did was bang on about myself. When Luke told me that your father had had a cardiac arrest, I thought that he was going to die and it would be too late then to say to you that I was sorry for the way I've been.'

'You crazy, crazy lady.' He was smiling but his eyes were brimming as he spoke.

She buried her face in his chest but he pulled her up, holding her chin in his hand.

'Look at me, Fleur. Look at me and listen to what I have to say. We had a row, a silly row, that is all. Do you really think I would throw away all that we have together because of a few harsh words? Yes, I was angry, but it doesn't mean for one moment that I stopped loving you.'

For a second she double took. 'You love me?'

'Yes, Fleur, I love you. I think I've loved you right from that day at Auskick. Before that even, like when you tried to poison me with salt. But it had to be right, Fleur. We both had to be so very sure. Alex is too precious to be hurt again and so are you. The only reason I didn't tell you about my father in the end was because I truly thought you'd had enough bad news for one day. I thought it would keep for another time. I didn't realise then that I would have to rush off so quickly. I tried to ring you as soon as I heard the bad news, you must believe me.'

'I was at my mother-in law's,' Fleur admitted. 'And I didn't get home till late. You'd have already been on the plane. I just thought you were gone for good, that I'd never get a chance—'

'But I would have come back. Teresa is not flying out until the weekend. I told her to let you know what was happening. Why didn't you ask her?'

'It would have been a lot simpler,' Fleur admitted.

'But a lot less romantic,' Mario said tenderly. 'Look at me,' he insisted again as her eyes dropped down to her bitten nails. 'I was never going to leave things there. I was always going to come back to you.'

'But what if he'd died, what if you couldn't have—?'

'I would have found a way. Fleur, my father has been sick for years and, like most doctors, he ignored his symptoms. In a strange way this is the best thing that could have ever happened. He has had a quadruple bypass and, yes, he is sick but he is recovering, and now he has years left in him. The last forty-eight hours have been hellish, I admit that, but seeing you here, knowing you did this for me, well, it makes up for it a thousand times over.'

His hand stroked her cheeks and she could feel the warmth of his body spreading through her own. She wanted to be comforted, wanted to believe it was all that easy but there were still too many questions.

'What about Alex? I can't ask him to come here...'

'Nor will you have to.'

'But your parents—'

'Will be fine,' he finished for her. 'They can come to Australia for my father's recuperation, and spend some time getting to know you and Alex. Or maybe we can all fly out to Italy in a few months for a holiday.'

She looked at him then, really looked. The sapphire of his eyes were bright with love and finally Fleur dared to hope, but then those eyes suddenly darkened. Taking her hand, he turned it over slowly.

'You've taken off your rings.'

Fleur swallowed, 'I didn't know what to do,' she stated honestly. 'It just seemed wrong somehow to be wearing them when I was coming to tell you this. I put them in my handbag,' she finished lamely.

Tenderly Mario pulled her towards him, soothing her with a gentle kiss. 'My beautiful Fleur, I know how hard this must be for you. I thought of your rings, too.'

'You did?' She gazed up at him. 'Really?'

Tipping her gently off his knee, he stood up. She sensed his trepidation. Sensed the enormity of what was coming.

'I'm not very good at this either. If I say the wrong thing now, or I upset you, know that was never my intention. Please, understand it is because I am nervous.'

Fleur nodded, watching as he took a long dark purple box out of his pocket. 'That night when I came to find you, I brought this with me. I thought leaving you with these might show my commitment to you. I don't know if this is the right solution but, please, hear what I have to say.'

His normally steady hands were trembling as he undid the clasp and Fleur felt her eyes fill as she stared down at the delicate gold chain nestled in the soft dark velvet, a huge ruby ring lying in the centre. 'When I bought this ring for you, as I said, I thought about your rings also. Maybe we are on the same wave distance?'

'Length,' she said, unable to help herself, unable to grasp the magnitude of his insight.

'I don't want to take away your memories, Fleur, I just want to give you new ones, good ones. Rory is a part of you. He gave you your beautiful child, he helped make you the wonderful woman you are today. And though he is gone he is still here, loving you, taking care of you, and hopefully he would approve of me. Don't hide your rings away. Perhaps you could wear them on this chain, keep him close to your heart.'

Two huge tears splashed from her eyes onto the velvet. 'I have said the wrong thing, yes? It was stupid of me…'

Fleur shook her head, wiping the tears away with the back of her hand. 'No, Mario, it was the nicest thing you could possibly have done.' And as she placed the rings on the chain and Mario rather clumsily fiddled with the clasp as she held her hair up, Fleur knew then, without a shadow of doubt, that Mario Ruffini was the man she would spend the rest of her life with.

As he slipped his ring onto her finger she realised that the bad days were behind her now. The lonely nights, the fear, the guilt, they were all finally over.

'You mean you'll live in Australia for ever?'

'How could I not?' he said huskily. 'How could I bear to leave you behind again? Anyway, you'd just get on a plane and follow me.'

She nestled into him, closing her eyes as he held her ever closer, finally allowing herself to be comforted, to accept the future with Mario there beside her.

'Australia will be our home,' he whispered gently, chasing away any last shadows of doubt as golden rays of hope shone in. 'After all, wasn't it you, Fleur, who taught me that home is where the heart is?'

EPILOGUE

Is THERE a master plan to it all? Do the ones we love live on after they've died, sending us signs, letting us know that it is OK to go on living, to go on loving, even after they've gone?

It was a question Fleur had pondered long and hard. Only this night when she awoke the questions ran deeper. Glancing over to the alarm clock, she watched as the hands crept past midnight and her birthday dawned. Her fourth without Rory and her first with Mario, her husband, by her side.

She felt Mario's hands pull her nearer, instinctively reaching for her swollen stomach and caressing her gently in his sleep. Massaging their unborn child, reassuring the anxious mother. How lucky she had been to find him, to go to bed each night beside him, to wake up each morning feeling held and cherished. Under his loving care she had watched Alex blossom, herself, too. A happy, contented family awaiting the newest addition in just three short weeks.

Restless, unsettled, she tried to relax, to drift back to sleep, but she couldn't. Slipping out of his embrace, she levered herself slowly out of bed. Perhaps some warm milk might help her unwind.

Passing the lounge, Fleur hesitated. Padding over to the photo of her and Rory, she stood a moment. How she wished he could see how Alex was doing, the fine boy he was, growing in confidence each day as the world opened up for him. Rory was Daddy, Mario Dad. Alex had been the one who'd suggested it, and Fleur had agreed to it, but it had been Mario who'd cried with love and pride the first time he'd heard Alex shyly say the magical word.

'I'm happy, darling. Alex is happy, too. You'd be so proud of him.'

How many times had she stood there waiting for a sign, for something to indicate that her Rory was feeling safe and loved, too? Maybe it was just a coincidence, maybe it had nothing to do with the date, but Fleur knew as the first contraction gripped her that the stars had somehow aligned, and that finally, after all this time, her message had been heaven-sent.

'Fleur?' Mario's voice was uncertain. Watching his precious wife doubled up, at first he thought she was crying. He didn't want to intrude, he knew this day was for her and Rory, yet he couldn't bear to see her crying alone in the dark.

'I think you'd better ring Kathy.' Straightening up, Fleur looked to where he stood, watching as realisation dawned.

'But you're not due for another three weeks.'

As another contraction gripped her he crossed the room. Taking her weight, he held her against him, rubbing her shoulders until it had passed.

'Try telling that to the baby.'

'Can I do anything? Tell me what you want me to do.'

She heard the anxiety in his voice and the tremor of excitement, too. They had waited so long for this moment yet still it had managed to take them by surprise.

'Turn on the shower for me and then ring Kathy. Greg's not working tonight, so Kathy can come over. We won't have to wake Alex. And ring the hospital to let them know.'

As meticulous as ever, Fleur had been ready for this moment for weeks now. Her bag was packed and waiting by the bedroom door. Kathy had been briefed that she would either be coming here or they would go to her, depending on Greg's shift. The car was constantly topped up with petrol. Nothing had been left to chance, nothing had been overlooked. Except, that was, that this baby might want to make a rapid appearance, a very rapid appearance.

As Fleur stepped under the shower she felt the tightening of another contraction, growing in intensity. Gasping, concentrating, she turned so the hot water hit her lower back, the strong jets providing welcome relief. And just when she thought it had passed, Fleur felt a gush as her waters broke. It all happened so quickly, but, just as she knew the shower would have to wait, that they needed to get to the hospital quickly, Fleur was suddenly hit with an overwhelming urge, a desperate need to push.

'Mario,' she called urgently. 'Mario.' And she sank to the floor. As he rushed back into the *en suite*, for a second she wished she had a camera handy so she could capture his terrified features as he watched his wife grimacing with the effort of not pushing.

'It's coming,' she gasped. 'We're not going to make it to the hospital.'

Terror was in her voice this time and Mario heard it. He stood, stunned, for a second. Never mind the hospital. They weren't even going to make it back to the bed! Already he could see the thick, dark hair of his child.

He was beside her in an instant. 'Who needs the hospital when we have each other?'

Turning off the shower, he knelt before her. His hands reaching down, he felt a rush of love as he watched nature unfold. All he had to do was guide the tiny head and tell Fleur over and over how wonderful she was, how well she was doing.

'I want to scream,' she said through clenched teeth. 'I'll scare Alex.'

'Scream, darling,' he reassured her. 'Alex will be fine.'

She let go then, gave in to the urge, listened to her body. As her scream filled the night air it was replaced in a moment with the lusty cries of their daughter, yelling with indignation at her rapid entry into the world.

They held each other for a moment, crying, gazing in awe at the miracle of birth.

'Fleur!' Kathy rushed into the room. 'Oh, my God!' Whipping the doona off the bed, she wrapped it around the stunned trio.

'What took you so long?' Fleur asked, her eyes not leaving her infant.

Only when Alex stumbled in, his pyjamas creased, his blond hair sticking up, rubbing sleep from his eyes as he took in the scene before him, did Fleur look up, holding an arm out to her son.

'Come here, darling, come and meet your baby sister.'

'I heard screaming,' he said, utterly bewildered.

Mario pulled him in, wrapping his arm around his entire family as Kathy cried openly.

'That was because she arrived so quickly, Alex,' he said gently. 'She was in a rush to meet her big brother.'

They had a cuddle, but not for long. When Fleur started to shiver and the impracticality of the four of them huddled in the shower started to surface, Mario gave her a kiss. 'How about we settle you into bed and I'll ring the hospital?'

Fleur nodded gratefully.

'Will she still have to go?' Alex asked, his eyes looking anxiously from his sister to his mother.

'I think it would be better,' Mario said gently. 'Mum needs a little time to rest, and you and I can get the house ready for when they both come home. We still need to set up the crib.'

It wasn't till they were tucked up in bed with a welcome cup of tea and a swaddle of warm blankets that the date suddenly registered.

'It's your birthday, Mum.'

'So it is.' Fleur looked down at her new daughter, her eyes as blue and knowing as her father's. 'Which means it's this little lady's birthday, too.'

Was it a sign? Was it Rory's way of giving his blessing, of telling her that he understood, that it really was time to finally be happy?

Over the years Alex had seen his mother's pain on this day, however hard Fleur had tried to hide it. But today, as he lay in his mum's and dad's arms with his new sister sweet and warm next to him, he reached over and kissed the newborn baby and then his mother. 'It really is a happy birthday this time, isn't it, Mum?'

The tears that rolled down Fleur's cheeks held no grief or sadness. They were tears of pure joy.

'Yes, darling,' she whispered, as Mario held her tighter. 'This time it really is a happy birthday.'

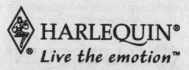

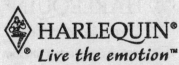

The world's bestselling romance series.

HARLEQUIN®
Presents~

Seduction and Passion Guaranteed!

MILLIONAIRE MARRIAGES
When the million-dollar question is "Will you marry me?"

**Coming Soon in Harlequin Presents...
An exciting duet by talented author**

Sandra Field

Don't miss...

May 2004: The Millionaire's Marriage Demand #2395
Julie Renshaw is shocked when Travis Strathern makes an outrageous demand: marriage! She is overwhelmingly attracted to him—but is she ready to marry him for convenience? Travis is used to getting his own way—but Julie makes certain he won't this time...unless their marriage is based on love as well as passion....

June 2004: The Tycoon's Virgin Bride #2401
One night Jenessa's secret infatuation with tycoon Bryce Laribee turned to passion—but the moment he discovered she was a virgin he walked out! Twelve years later, the attraction between them is just as mind-blowing, and Bryce is determined to finish what they started. But Jenessa has a secret or two....

Available wherever Harlequin books are sold.

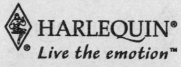

HARLEQUIN®
Live the emotion™

Visit us at www.eHarlequin.com

HPMILMAR

The world's bestselling romance series.

HARLEQUIN®
Presents

Seduction and Passion Guaranteed!

OUTBACK KNIGHTS
Marriage is their mission!

From bad boys—to powerful,
passionate protectors!

Three tycoons from the Outback
rescue their brides-to-be....

**Coming soon in Harlequin Presents:
Emma Darcy's exciting new trilogy**

Meet Ric, Mitch and Johnny—once three Outback bad
boys, now rich and powerful men. But these sexy city
tycoons must return to the Outback to face a new
challenge: claiming their women as their brides!

**MAY 2004: THE OUTBACK MARRIAGE RANSOM #2391
JULY 2004: THE OUTBACK WEDDING TAKEOVER #2403
NOVEMBER 2004: THE OUTBACK BRIDAL RESCUE #2427**

*"Emma Darcy delivers a spicy love story...
a fiery conflict and a hot sensuality."
—Romantic Times*

Available wherever Harlequin books are sold.

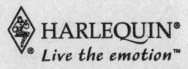

HARLEQUIN®
Live the emotion™

Visit us at www.eHarlequin.com